GREYSTONE HEARTS

A Novel

Second Edition

Linda Kay DuBose

Greystone Hearts is entirely fictional. Any resemblance to actual events, persons or places is purely coincidental. Names of actual people mentioned in passing are used simply to give credit where credit is due.

No part of this book may be reproduced, stored in a retrieval system, or transmitted by any means without the written permission of the author.

First published by CrossBooks - 9/15/2011
This edition contains minor revisions to the original paperback edition.

Certain book cover stock imagery © by Fotolia
(Used by permission/purchase)

Copyright © 2016 by Linda Kay DuBose

ISBN-13: 978-1533597632
ISBN-10: 1533597634

For Wayne

My husband
of forty-eight years

My best friend

The love of my life

Also by Linda Kay DuBose

ERVE AND LIZZIE (historical fiction)

SOMEDAY, MAYBE…FOR SURE!

EMERALD MIST

ACKNOWLEDGEMENTS

Thank you, Heavenly Father, for the opportunity to do what I enjoy.

Thank you, Wayne, for continuing to be my faithful husband, my greatest fan and the enthusiastic supporter of all my ventures.

Thank you, Jean Basham, for your continued friendship and for wading through the murky waters of my first draft and offering suggestions and encouragement.

Thank you, Officer Larry Pitts, of the Mobile, AL, Police Department, for your law enforcement perspective and expertise.

Thank you, daughter-in-law Alicia DuBose, for your thorough scouring of the final manuscript for editoral adjustments.

Thank you, Ronnie Basham, for updating the book cover for this second edition.

FORGIVENESS
By LKD

Record injustice in the sand,
In time, 'tis waft away.
Carve a blessing deep in stone,
Despite the winds, 'twill stay.

"He who is greedy is always in want."

(A quote from the Roman lyric poet, Horace)

CHAPTER 1

Josh, twenty years old, elder brother to Mark, sat at the dining room table, typing away on his laptop, deeply engrossed in finishing a term paper. He was mid-way through his junior year as a history major at Halford Easterling College. He looked forward to graduating and becoming a high school coach and history teacher. Easterling didn't have a football team, but they had a cracker-jack baseball team, and baseball was the sport of choice for Josh. In addition to baseball and history, Josh's third passion was classical guitar. All who heard him play recognized that he'd been given a special musical gift, and he had worked hard to develop his talent.

Josh's mom was an elementary schoolteacher, and she often reminded him that many teachers have to find a way to supplement their incomes. Josh would be able to do that by teaching guitar lessons and playing for special events. He and Mark already played together at church functions, weddings and community affairs. Mark was equally gifted at the piano and extremely accomplished for his age.

Unlike a lot of young people, Josh didn't struggle with trying to decide what to do with his life. He always seemed to know, from the time he was a kid, what his talents and interests were and where his life was headed. But, for the moment, he was focused on getting his term paper completed. His subject was "The Impact of Thomas Jefferson on American History," and the paper was due to be turned in by three o'clock on Friday. It was now Thursday evening, and procrastination was demanding payment.

Mark, his younger brother, had been upstairs completing his own school assignments. He was a junior in high school, the proud new owner of a driver's license and becoming very interested in a certain young lady from church named Natalie. Natalie worked a short shift in the evenings on Tuesdays and Thursdays and a full shift on Saturdays at the most popular hangout for the teens in the community, the Gator Drive-In, boasting the best "build-it-yourself" burgers in the county. Mark particularly loved cheeseburgers and especially craved them on Tuesdays, Thursdays, and Saturdays!

"What kind of meeting did Mom and Dad have tonight?" Mark inquired of his studious older brother as he bounded down the steps, finally free from his scholastic obligations for the evening.

"Adult Sunday School Department fellowship," Josh mumbled, not bothering to look up from his work.

"I'm starved!" Mark announced.

"What's new?" Josh replied, pausing just long enough to think what a bottomless pit Mark's stomach was known to be and to wonder how he remained such a bean pole, considering how much and how often he ate.

"Hey, let's go to the Gator Drive-In and get a cheeseburger and some fries," Mark proposed hopefully.

"Can't do it, buddy . . . got too much work to do. Besides, Mom left a tuna casserole and some English peas in the fridge for us to warm up for supper. She said it's a new casserole recipe and that you'll like this one better than the last one."

"Aw, man! You know I can't stand tuna casserole. Can't you just take a break for half an hour?"

"Wish I could, bro, but you know it would stretch into at least an hour, and I'm going to be up most of the night as it is. Just fix yourself a peanut butter and jelly sandwich and a glass of milk. Besides, you'll see Natalie at school tomorrow!"

"Who said anything about Natalie?" Mark objected. "I can't help it if she happens to work where I like to eat!" Mark, bashful about his attraction to Natalie, protested the implication.

"Look, kid, you work it out with your stomach. I've got to get back to **my** work. Sorry!" Josh attempted to close the conversation.

Not willing to give up just yet, Mark offered another plan. "Hey, I've got my license . . . had it a month now. Why can't I go by myself? It's only about two miles from here, and I'll drive extra careful!"

"Nah, I don't think so." Josh, losing patience, sighed heavily. "Mom and Dad don't want you driving at night yet. I just can't let you do it."

"Aw, come on, Josh! You know I'm a good driver. I promise I won't go over thirty miles an hour all the way, and I'll be home in an hour, and I'll bring you a cheeseburger, and I'll be back long before Mom and Dad get home. They'll never even know, and I'll be out of your hair while you work," Mark pled relentlessly as he playfully yanked a strand of Josh's hair to emphasize his last point.

"Oh, for Pete's sake, do what you want to do! But if you go and Mom and Dad find out, you'll have to answer to them. You'd better think about it. Now, please, let me get back to work!"

With the decision placed squarely on his own shoulders, Mark paused a minute to think. He walked into the kitchen, opened the fridge and glared at the ugly, cold casserole sitting there, seeming to stare back at him. *Nothing personal, just can't handle you tonight!* Mark thought as he shut the door on the tuna and turned to look at the clock on the kitchen wall.

Seven o'clock. No way they'll be home before nine. I could slip out the back door, take Mom's car, and be back here no later than eight-fifteen. If I don't tell Josh I'm going, he won't have to worry about me. Chances are I'll be back before he misses me. Natalie gets off at eight. Maybe I could even take her home.

Mark shuffled around in the kitchen for a couple of minutes, clanging and clattering some dishes, opening and closing the fridge, making noises as though he were going to eat in . . . just in case Josh were paying attention. Then, he quietly took his mom's car keys off the key peg, slipped out the back door and got into the car.

The car was an eleven-year-old Nissan Maxima that still ran pretty well. The mileage was high, and the paint job rather faded . . . not exactly the car he'd like to be driving in order to impress Natalie, but it would, as they say, get him from point *a* to point *b*. Fortunately, Mom's car was parked in the driveway instead of the garage, lessening the chances that Josh would hear the motor crank. Mark grinned as he carefully backed out of the driveway and headed south on Franklin Street, toward the Gator Drive-In. *One cheeseburger . . . ketchup, mustard, heavy on the pickles . . . a large order of fries and a medium Dr. Pepper . . . coming right up, and Natalie too!*

CHAPTER 2

If one must write a term paper, it was good to have an interesting subject. For a history buff, the study of Thomas Jefferson offered a plethora of information. Few people in history were as proficient in as many different activities and studies as Jefferson. Josh was duly impressed and immersed in the intrigue of Jefferson's life. How was he going to condense his findings into a mere two thousand words?

Time had slipped away unnoticed since Josh had last spoken to Mark on the subject of supper. At about eight fifteen, he was aroused from his focus on Jefferson by a rap at the front door. Unexpected visitors at the pastor's home were not uncommon, and as he stepped toward the door Josh was hoping that this would not be one of those interruptions that ruined his work plans and would cost him additional hours of sleep.

Upon opening the door, he found Reggie Green, in uniform, standing solemnly on the porch. Reggie was a city policeman who lived in the neighborhood, just three doors down, and although he and his family belonged to another church, they occasionally visited Josh's church. The Greens were great neighbors and good friends.

"Hey, man, come on in!" Josh welcomed Reggie with no qualms because he often stopped by for a brief visit. But as Josh looked into Reggie's face he began to realize that this visit was different. Panic started to swell up in Josh's chest. "What's wrong? Are my parents okay? What's happened?" Before Officer Green could enter the house, another family friend came running across the yard and up onto the porch. He was the youth minister from Josh's church, Thomas Allen. He, too, wore a grave expression.

"Your parents are okay, Josh," Reggie continued. "They'll be here shortly. I do have some bad news, but I'll wait until they get here to talk about it."

"Is it somebody from the church . . . a friend of ours? Do I need to go upstairs and get Mark?" Josh continued to question.

Reggie and Thomas gave each other a puzzled look. "No, Josh, it won't be necessary to call Mark. Let's wait for your folks. I think that's their car pulling in right now."

David and Lydia Williams, Josh's parents, hurried to join the others on the porch. They searched the officer's face for signs of hope and held their breath, knowing they may be about to hear the worst news they could imagine. They had received a call at the church telling them to go home immediately because there had been an accident involving a family member. What kind of accident, where, when, how or how bad they were not told. They were trying to brace themselves for the worst, but were puzzled by the fact that Josh was standing there, seemingly fine, and Mark must be there as well, perhaps upstairs watching television. Neither had notice that the Maxima was missing from the far end of the driveway. Obviously, the person involved in an accident was from their extended family . . . a parent, sister or brother, aunt or uncle, cousin. The tension of waiting to find out what was going on caused them to tremble inwardly.

"Bro. Williams, Mrs. Lydia, let's go in and sit down a minute. I need to talk to you inside." As Officer Green escorted the family and the youth minister into the house, other friends were beginning to arrive and congregate on the lawn. Thomas turned and asked the group to wait outside for a few minutes and allow the family some privacy while they heard from Officer Green.

"Josh, go get your brother," Lydia instructed as they each took a seat in the living room.

"No, Josh," Reggie spoke gently while reaching out and stopping Josh as he turned in the direction of the stairs. "Mark isn't here."

"What do you mean, he isn't here? Of course he's here! Where else would he be?" Josh responded in bewilderment. But as soon as he asked the question, he knew the answer. Everything was beginning to come clear. Mark had left the house, gone to the Gator Drive-In, and something terrible had happened to him. "Oh, dear God, what's happened to my brother?" Josh fell limply into the big, over-stuffed chair beside the sofa on which his parents were sitting. He bowed his head, rested his elbows on his knees and buried his face in his hands, unable to look at anyone as Officer Green, their friend, sympathetically and tenderly broke the news to them of Mark's accident.

As the story unfolded, it was interrupted from time to time with the sobs and anguished cries of the shocked and heartbroken family. Basically, they were told that Mark had been on his way down Franklin Street, headed south. According to several witnesses, he stopped at a red light, waited for it to turn green and then proceeded to cross the intersection. A speeding car going west on Juniper Avenue ran the red light and hit Mark's car so hard the force of the collision drove the Maxima through the plate-glass window of a children's clothing store located on the corner. Mark was apparently killed instantly.

The other vehicle was traveling at a speed in excess of eighty miles an hour in a business and residential area where the speed limit was thirty-five miles per hour. The driver was a twenty-one-year-old male with prior arrests for DUI who was fleeing from the police. A policeman had tried to pull him over for running a stop sign and reckless driving, suspecting that he was drunk or under the influence of drugs. The young man was apparently determined not to be arrested. Reggie stopped the account at that point, knowing what the first question to follow would be, once this much had been comprehended.

Amidst their sobs David asked, "What's the condition of the other driver?"

"He has only minor cuts, abrasions, and bruises. He was treated at the scene and has been arrested and taken to jail," Reggie replied.

The next questions cut Josh to the core. "Josh, why was Mark out in the car? Where was he going? Didn't you know where he was?" Lydia begged an explanation from him.

Josh shook as he tried to control his crying and get his words out. "Mom, he wanted a cheeseburger from the Gator Drive-In. I told him not to go, to eat the casserole or make a sandwich. I thought that was what he was doing when he left me typing my term paper in the dining room. I thought he ate his supper and went back upstairs. I never knew he left the house. I told him you didn't want him driving at night. I'm so sorry. I didn't know. I just didn't know!"

Josh's parents rose to embrace him as the three of them gave way to their anguish and wept bitterly in each other's arms. Thomas and Reggie began to pray fervently and audibly over the grieving threesome for God to give them strength to bear their loss and to guide and comfort them in the days ahead.

After a while, Officer Green said, "I think you've gotten all the information you can digest for tonight, except that Mark's body is being respectfully tended to at the morgue, and in the morning you can start to make arrangements with the funeral home. I'll be back to check on you tomorrow. In the meantime, call me if there's anything I can do for you." With those words, he left and invited the friends and family waiting outside to go in and be with the Williams family in their hour of great need.

All through the long, exhausting, sleepless night, amidst the crying, talking, praying and whispering of the family and close friends who remained, certain words resounded and pounded in Josh's mind, *Can't do it, buddy . . . got too much work to do . . . for Pete's sake, do what you want to do . . . please, let me get back to work. . . . Oh, dear God, it's my fault!*

CHAPTER 3

Officer Winston Reeves would never forget the events of that night. He had been traveling west on Juniper Avenue in his squad car when he noticed that the car up ahead was weaving in and out of its lane. He followed a little closer to see if the problem continued. When the driver got to the four-way stop at Juniper Avenue and Douglas Street, he never even touched his brake. Winston turned on his flashing light and sounded a couple of blasts from his siren to signal the driver to pull over, but, instead, the driver gunned it and left the squad car in his exhaust fumes. Reeves followed in hot pursuit but soon realized that, although he could probably hang with the guy and eventually pull him over, a very dangerous situation was developing. He slowed down and radioed in a description of the vehicle and instructed fellow officers in the area to be on the lookout.

Reeves knew that car, an instantly recognizable Corvette, and its driver. The officer realized that the driver was headed in the direction of his favorite watering hole, most likely planning to drink himself into a stupor, as was his habit. It would be much safer to follow him at a distance and arrest him there. Reeves could only hope that the guy would slow down and either be intercepted by another officer or get to his destination without hurting anyone. But the fleeing driver didn't slow down, and Reeves heard the horrific sound of colliding metal, squealing tires, and shattering glass a block away as he approached the intersection of Juniper and Franklin. His worst fear had materialized in mere seconds. He was the first officer on the scene. Reggie Green was the second.

About forty-five minutes later, most of the bystanders had dispersed and were going on about their business, albeit with disturbing images fixed in their minds. It was not likely that they would ever forget what they had seen and heard that fateful evening. Some of them knew, or knew of, the Williams family. Most knew, or knew of, the other young man and his family.

The driver of the Corvette was Bradley Clemons Jr. He was the troubled, spoiled, disorderly twenty-one-year-old son of Bradley Clemons Sr., arguably the most prominent, wealthy, and powerful businessman in town. It was no secret that "Junior" had been in and out of trouble from childhood. Nor was it a secret that his dad had covered for him and bailed him out of trouble with the law and other authorities several times. No one knew what a problem Junior had, and was, more than his former teachers. Because of the power and manipulation of his father, they had not been able to take measures to discipline him and teach him to respect authority. They had simply rejoiced at the end of each school year when they were able to promote him on to the next grade level and look forward to a less stressful year to follow. Since his high school graduation, Junior had done little or nothing to better himself, living at home and sponging off his doting parents. He had started college classes, twice, and dropped out both times. His drinking problem had gotten worse, and his life was totally out of control.

But even knowing the senior and junior Clemonses as they did, the bystanders were totally unprepared to handle the pair's reaction to the accident. A handful of folks had gathered near Junior as paramedics checked him out and dressed his minor injuries. They were there when Junior's dad arrived and breathlessly ran to his son's side, relieved to see that he was all right. They overheard the conversation between father and son as Junior whined and cried about having totaled his beloved Corvette with its "souped-up" engine and new custom paint job, unlike any other in town. Their stomachs turned as he complained that the cops had it in for him and carped that this was that cop's fault for chasing him. He made no mention of the other driver's death.

Bradley Sr. attempted to calm him by promising to replace the car. "Don't worry, son," he consoled. "We'll get you a new one, and we can soup it up and paint it up any way you want it. Now stop blubbering and pull yourself together. Right now we've got more to worry about than your car. The cops are going to want to question you, but you keep your mouth shut. I'm calling my attorney, and we're not going to say a word until we talk to him first. You just leave this to me. I'll take care of everything."

Clemons had been unaware that Officer Reggie Green was among the group of people standing nearby. Green had been gathering information from those who had witnessed the accident. He also overheard the discussion between father and son. Taking a deep breath and struggling to control his anger, Reggie stepped forward, notebook in hand, and began to question Junior.

"Young man, if you're the driver of that Corvette, I need to get your statement as to how this accident occurred," he began.

Forgetting his instructions already, Junior opened his mouth, his breath reeking of alcohol, and started to answer. Quickly, his dad stepped between his son and Officer Green.

"My son has nothing to say without our lawyer present," he firmly declared.

"Mr. Clemons, your son is not under arrest just yet. I'm only trying to fill out an accident report at the moment, and, as you may or may not know, the other driver can't answer questions. He's dead. I would appreciate your co-operation!" Reggie responded, using all his resolve to remain professional.

"Well, it's too bad about the other boy, Officer, but I have my own son's welfare to think about," Clemons coolly responded.

Unable to contain his disgust, Officer Green replied, "Well, it's nice for you that you have your son's **welfare** to think about. David and Lydia Williams will have their son's **funeral** to think about!"

With that, Officer Green slapped his notebook shut and walked away. He turned the questioning over to his fellow officers and stepped into the shadows, alone, to weep. He had to prepare himself for the task facing him. He should be the one to tell Mark's family. *After all,* he thought, *what are friends for?*

CHAPTER 4

Greystone Community Church was packed with people attending Mark's funeral service. Mark was well liked at his high school by both students and teachers. Josh had many friends from college who came to show their respects. Lydia had a vast circle of friends, fellow teachers, students and parents from the school where she had taught for over ten years. They turned out in great numbers.

And, of course, the entire family was near and dear to the congregation they had served for almost fifteen years. These people had watched Josh and Mark grow up and had a powerful hand in helping them develop into the fine young men they were. Pastor Williams had been the one to preach and teach the Word to them faithfully, to marry their young, to rejoice over their newborns, counsel their problems, baptize their converts, visit and pray for the sick, bury their dead and try to comfort them in their grief. Now it was the congregation's turn to minister to their minister and his family. They did not fail.

As though it were not enough to deal with the loss of their son and brother, the Williamses now had to deal with the wrongness of their tragedy . . . the fact that another person's recklessness and disregard for the safety of others had caused Mark's death. Daily they begged the Lord to help them deal with the anger and bitterness trying to take root in their hearts as the reality of never seeing Mark again this side of heaven set in and filled them with loneliness and sorrow. They had preached and practiced forgiveness and love for many years, but they were beginning to believe there was a limit to what they could forgive and to whom they could show love.

Junior Clemons had rocked their world, broken their hearts, and, if allowed to, could shake their faith in God and in justice. They wrestled day and night with the age-old question, "Why do the righteous suffer while the wicked seem to prosper?" Not that they considered themselves "righteous" in their own eyes. They knew they were imperfect, but they had been made righteous in the eyes of God through the blood of Christ their Savior, and they tried, with God's help, to live clean, lawful, responsible lives that would honor Christ and help others.

The Clemonses, on the other hand, appeared to live for themselves alone. Bradley Clemons was known for his stinginess and harshness with his employees. He had stepped on and wounded many who he considered to be "little people" in his climb up the business ladder to financial success. Most of Clemons' "friendships" were not formed out of mutual fondness and trust, but out of intimidation, bribery and common ambitions. Bradley only gave of himself and his considerable wealth when it might be beneficial to him. Bradley and Janice Clemons spoiled and lavished on their children the very best of everything. And yet, their son walked away practically unscathed from the accident he had caused. Where was the justice in that?

Junior was locked away now, convicted of vehicular homicide, DWI, driving without a license (which had been revoked for previous violations), reckless endangerment, and speeding. The normal range of sentencing for first degree vehicular homicide, a felony, was three to fifteen years in prison with a mandatory one year of time served. In light of his previous record, everyone expected Junior to serve at least five years. When Judge Atwater was appointed to the case, folks felt encouraged because they knew Atwater to be a fair-minded judge. He was not considered unduly tough and heartless, nor was he seen as weak and soft on crime. And, he was a family man with teenagers of his own. He should be able to relate to the emotional impact of this tragedy on both families.

Junior remained in the local jail for roughly three weeks while awaiting his court date, which was scheduled for early in January. There was to be no trial per se. Junior intended to plead "no contest," but he had to appear before a judge to formally make his plea and to receive his sentencing.

On that day, Rev. Williams was given an opportunity to speak on behalf of his family. He was torn between the sorrow and anger he felt and the forgiveness and mercy he was expected, as a Christian minister, to extend to his son's killer. All he could bring himself to do, after much prayer, was to tell what a wonderful young man Mark had been, how deeply he was loved and how sadly he was missed. He told the judge he was not asking for vengeance, but for justice. He concluded by stating, "Junior Clemons is a troubled young man, and until his life is changed he will continue to be a danger to himself and to society. Our son had something very special that Junior does not appear to have. Mark had a personal relationship with Jesus Christ as his Savior. That's why his life was so good. That's why we know he's in heaven today. It is our prayer that Junior will come to know Christ as Mark did and be pardoned by the only One who can truly pardon sin, the Lord Jesus Christ."

"Bradley Clemons Jr., please stand," Judge Atwater ordered. All those in attendance as a show of support for the Williams family held their breath in anticipation of the judge's words. "Bradley Clemons Jr., you are hereby sentenced to three years in state prison. You will be required to serve one year of that sentence before the possibility of parole. If you are granted a parole after a year of imprisonment, you will then be placed on probation for a period not to exceed three years." Then, with the pounding of his gavel, Judge Atwater declared, "Court adjourned!" Rising immediately from his "lofty throne," the judge quickly headed to his side door exit. And that was that! No explanation, no comment to Junior on the seriousness of his offenses, and not a word of condolence to the Williamses. Period!

There was heard a collective gasp from the observers. Rev. and Mrs. Williams sat in stunned silence. Josh jumped to his feet and yelled, "What? That's all? Are you crazy? That's all my brother's death means to you?" The judge never looked back as he practically fled the scene. Josh's parents hastened to restrain Josh and to try to console him.

"Son, son, don't! It won't do any good, and it certainly won't bring Mark back," Lydia tearfully pled. "If he had received a life sentence, we'd be grieving and missing Mark just the same. We've got to let go of this and leave justice up to God. I know it doesn't seem like it, but He's in control, and He will deal with Junior Clemons according to His purposes." Those words articulated the faith of the Williamses, but not their feelings. Their emotions had a long way to travel to catch up with their faith.

In the following weeks and months, no one fully knew the battle raging within Josh as he grappled with his own sense of responsibility for the accident and the growing hatred he harbored for Junior

Clemons, the entire Clemons family, and the crooked judge. It was obvious to him that money had exchanged hands. The way he saw it, Junior was lying around reading, occasionally watching television, getting free "room and board" at tax-payer expense, exercising, and even getting free medical attention if and when needed while Josh and his family worked hard for what they had, in the grip of suffocating grief.

The Clemons family could go visit Junior regularly while Josh's family could only visit a grave in Greystone's Memory Garden Cemetery. And in only one year Junior would most likely be free to pick up his life where he had left it. He could continue on his merry way, enabled by his indulgent parents. His mom and dad would have their son back. David and Lydia Williams would never have their son back.

Josh's first semester teachers were understanding and accommodating. They had allowed him extended time to finish his required work and testing so that he could complete the semester over the Christmas holidays. Christmas had been totally depressing without Mark, and starting his second semester was something Josh did only at the urging of his parents and friends. He tried hard to keep up a good front, attending classes, doing his assignments, going to church, and playing first base on his college baseball team when baseball season rolled around again . . . going through the motions, mostly for the benefit of his parents. But, deep inside, trouble was brewing. Someday, somehow . . . the Clemons family and the judge they had purchased would pay. He would see to that.

CHAPTER 5

Somehow, Josh made it through the second semester, and now the summer loomed before him. He missed Mark even more because they had always enjoyed baseball, swimming, camping and fishing together in the summers.

Pastor and Mrs. Williams dealt with their grief by immersing themselves in more church activities. Staying busy ministering to others somehow helped facilitate their own healing. They encouraged Josh to take part in some of those activities, but he always found an excuse. They worried that he was turning inward, rather than upward and outward, to deal with his anger and loneliness.

It wasn't so much what he said or did that caused them concern, but more what he didn't say or do. Once as easy to read as an open book, they felt he was now concealing his true thoughts and feelings. Their conversations with Josh no longer flowed freely, and his responses seemed almost rehearsed. While he still attended church services on Sundays and Wednesday nights, he showed no real interest or enthusiasm as he once had. Everyone at the church was saddened to see him drop out of the praise band that helped lead worship on Sunday mornings. He hardly ever played his guitar at home any more, although he continued taking lessons. Occasionally, he would leave the house and be gone for hours without telling his parents where he was going. After returning, when they asked where he had been, he'd say he was just riding around town, or had gone to the city park to run on the public track. They had lost their younger son very suddenly. It seemed they were losing their older son gradually as he retreated emotionally into a shell.

Josh did not lie when he said he was riding around or running in the park. He was, indeed, doing a good bit of both. What he didn't reveal was his motive. Nor did he mention the time he spent visiting Mark's grave.

Because Greystone was a college town, summer jobs were not exactly plentiful. There were more students than available jobs. Josh had looked about for something to do that would help him pay his way. He didn't like being totally dependent on his parents. He had always found some type of work, at least part time, during the summers and saved up his money to help with his school expenses. That, plus the occasional small honorariums he received from playing guitar for special events kept him from feeling like a total moocher. But, at long last, he settled on a plan that would help him kill two birds with one stone. He would sign on with a lawn-service crew that worked in certain upscale communities. He could earn money, observe the activities of particular residents and look for the perfect opportunity to exact a little justice of his own.

"Mom, Dad, I've been offered a job with Cameron Lawn Service for the rest of the summer," Josh announced at the supper table one evening. "I think I'll take it. The pay's not great, and it's hot, hard work, but I think it will do me good to be busy and to be outdoors. What do you think?"

"Son, I like the idea very much," David responded, glad that Josh would have good physical labor to do that would help him work out his pent-up emotions.

Lydia was not quite as enthusiastic. "Josh, it gets awfully hot here in the summer. Are you sure you're physically up to working out in the heat all day? Couldn't you find an indoor job?"

"I tried, Mom. All the cushy jobs were taken first, I guess. But I really don't mind working outside. It should help keep me in shape. Besides, I know a couple of the guys on the crew, and I think I'd like to hang out with them this summer, even if it's just doing hard work together."

Convinced Josh was taking a positive step in dealing with the loss of Mark, she agreed. "That sounds like a good plan, son. Go for it."

*If you **knew** my plan, Mom, you wouldn't like it!* Josh thought.

~*~*~*~*~*~*~

"I'm gettin' a little fed up with this &%#@!" Bradley Clemons Sr. angrily announced as he threw the envelope containing the menacing drawing onto his desk. "When I find out who's behind this, I'm going to stuff every one of these stupid notes down his throat!"

Irately springing to his feet, Clemons thrust his rolling desk chair backwards with such force that it slammed into the expensive, designer drapes that covered the French doors behind him. As he lumbered across the floor toward the window, his wife, Janice, timidly picked up the envelope and peered inside. She removed the photocopy of a hand-sketched jail cell. Typed beneath the drawing were the words of a Longfellow poem, now quite familiar.

RETRIBUTION
Though the mills of God grind slowly,
Yet they grind exceeding small;
Though with patience He stands waiting,
With exactness grinds He all.

Janice was visibly troubled by the note and quickly placed this one with the others. They now had a collection numbering ten, each one exactly alike. Bradley had received one a week for ten straight weeks. The frustrating thing was that he had made so many enemies he couldn't accuse any one person of sending them. The scary thing was that the message could be more than wishful thinking or a benign warning. Someone may have discovered Bradley's most incriminating activities and may be threatening, in a veiled way, to spill the beans. Perhaps that someone was setting him up for blackmail. Or, was it something entirely different . . . a vengeful reference to Junior's incarceration?

"Bradley, what are you going to do about this?" Janice inquired.

"That's no business of yours! You just keep your nose out of it! The less you know about things, the better," Bradley snapped back at Janice. As usual, Janice recoiled from his rebuke and said nothing more about it.

The notes were definitely having their desired effect. Bradley, a man who for many years had used fear and intimidation to manipulate others, was learning how it felt to wear that shoe on the other foot.

CHAPTER 6

"Josh, telephone for you!" Lydia called up the staircase.

"Thanks, Mom. I'll take it up here!" Josh called back down the stairs.

"Hello . . . . Oh, hi, Mr. Murray . . . . Fine, thanks, and you? . . . . Oh, yes, sir! I really would be interested in talking to you about that . . . . Tomorrow morning at ten? . . . . Yes, sir, I'll be there. Thanks very much . . . good night." Josh hung up the phone and headed down the stairs with a spring in his step. Finally, something had happened that sparked some enthusiasm in his voice.

"Mom, Dad! That was Mr. Murray, my guitar teacher! You won't believe what he just told me! He's got more students signing up for lessons this year than he can handle. He wants to talk to me about taking some of the new ones and teaching them basic guitar! He wants me to come into Madison's tomorrow so we can work out some details and see if it's something I can fit into my school schedule." The words tumbled excitedly from his lips.

"That's great!" both parents responded at the same time. They were thrilled to see Josh's eagerness and began to ask him all sorts of questions he couldn't answer.

"That's all I know, but I'll find out more tomorrow. As soon as we finish our meeting, I'll call and fill you in on all the details. Boy, I sure hope it works out! After a summer of yard work, I'm ready for just about anything else, but to be able to start teaching guitar . . . now that would be awesome!"

Josh laid his head on his pillow that night and thanked God for the measure of joy he was experiencing as he thought about his future. He'd been spending so much time looking back, regretfully, that he seldom considered what good things could lie ahead for him. He wished he could tell Mark about his new job opportunity. In his heart he knew that Mark would want him to move on with his life and be happy.

Josh was ready to go long before ten o'clock on Saturday morning. He was going to meet Mr. Murray at Madison's Music Store. Madison's sold all sorts of printed music as well as pianos, keyboards, organs, and many other band and orchestral instruments. They also offered for rent several small studio spaces, located there in the Madison building, in which various music teachers could conduct their lessons.

Madison's was centrally located in the best part of downtown, making it an ideal location for its purpose. Inside, there was a nicely furnished seating area where parents could wait, if they wished, while their younger children were taking lessons. Josh had been taking classical guitar from Mr. Murray at Madison's for just over ten years and was quite familiar with the store, its owner, and its employees. He had established a very good rapport with the entire staff. He could not imagine a more desirable place to work.

Josh had to wait only a few minutes in the parents' seating area before Mr. Murray emerged from the studio he had used for roughly fifteen years, ever since he and his wife had moved to Greystone. Mr. Murray's primary job was to run the computer lab at Greystone Middle School, and he was a fabulous teacher of both computer skills and guitar.

More than that, he was a good man who cared about his students . . . the kind of man they could talk to and from whom they would receive wise counsel.

"Good morning, Josh! I'm sorry to get you out on the last Saturday morning before school begins again, but I'm really glad you're interested in my proposition. Why don't we step into the coffee shop next door and talk business?" Mr. Murray pushed open the heavy glass door and held it for Josh to exit before him. They chatted about little things . . . the weather, school starting, etc., until they were seated and each sipping on his own preferred type of caffeine. Then Mr. Murray began to lay out his plan.

"Josh, you may not be aware that my wife, Gwen, has had some health problems for a long time. In recent months, her condition has worsened to the point that I need to lighten my work load and spend as much time with her as I can. She's not very strong and needs extra care. It's somewhat complicated, but I've worked out a schedule with our two daughters, a couple of my wife's close friends, and hired-help so that I can continue my school job and teach guitar three afternoons and evenings during the week. However, I need to be with Gwen the other two weekday afternoons and evenings and on the weekends. I'll have to give up all my Saturday classes.

"I've spoken to my students and their parents and made arrangements to continue teaching my more advanced students on the three weekdays and to reserve Saturdays for the beginners and less advanced. If I can't find a good teacher for those Saturday students, they will be left with few options. I'd feel like I was abandoning them. But I've trained you, and you're my star student. I'm confident that you're well-qualified to begin teaching. I know that you'd give these beginners and intermediates a good foundation with proper technique that would not have to be corrected when they reach advanced levels. Who knows? This could be the beginning of a permanent arrangement for you. You're catching up to your old teacher's skills very quickly. I have no doubt you will surpass me, and that makes me proud. You make me look good!"

Josh hung his head, humbled by Mr. Murray's praise. Mr. Murray continued, "Right now I have six beginner students wanting lessons on Saturdays. You and their parents could work out a schedule, and you owe me nothing for their referral. You would, however, have to pick up the tab for the use of the studio I've reserved, but only for the hours you actually use it. It's a flat hourly fee that you'd pay directly to Madison's, and they are holding that room for you if you want it. You won't make a fortune, but you will earn enough to allow you to take a pretty girl out on a date now and then, and you'll be establishing yourself in the music community." Mr. Murray grinned broadly as he added the latter incentives. Josh was grinning, too. He liked the plan!

"Mr. Murray, I'm really sorry that your wife is ill, and I certainly hope she regains her health very soon. If I can help you and help your students in the meantime, I would love doing that. I'm flattered that you have confidence enough in me to give me this opportunity. But do you think the students and the parents will be willing to settle for me after having had the best? Those are some big shoes they'll be expecting me to fill."

"Oh, well, thanks for the compliment, Josh, but I feel sure they'll be more than pleased when I explain the situation and when I get through boasting about my prize pupil! As soon as I have your approval, I can put it to them and let them decide. Frankly, though, there's a shortage of good guitar teachers in our area, especially of the classical variety, and I believe most of the parents, if not all of them, will be more than willing to give it a try. And, once they do, I've no doubt they'll be completely satisfied! What do you say?"

"I say *yes!*" Josh enthusiastically replied. He could hardly wait to prove himself worthy of his teacher's trust, and he was eager to share the good news with his parents.

Half an hour later, after getting some basic information about his potential new students, Josh thanked Mr. Murray again for the opportunity and walked briskly to his car, dialing home on his cell phone as he walked. For no reason at all, he glanced back at Madison's, his new place of employment, just in time to see her. She was walking into Madison's, alone. *Amazing!* Josh thought. *I've looked for her all summer, and she shows up now!* Seeing her reminded him of the plan he had formulated at the beginning of summer and his commitment to seeing it through. Here was his opportunity to proceed.

CHAPTER 7

Josh waited in his car for the girl to come out of Madison's. Fifteen minutes later she emerged with a package in her hands. It appeared that she had purchased a music book, probably for piano. He had heard that she was the pianist in her church. Josh jumped out of his car and raced down the sidewalk to overtake her.

"Marci, wait up a minute!" he called out as he approached. "I need to talk to you."

Marci looked back, startled. "No . . . no, I'm sorry. I can't talk right now. I've got to get home." She picked up her pace. Josh did too.

"Marci, please, I just need a few minutes. Please, talk to me," he pled.

Marci never looked back. She nervously unlocked the car door with her remote gadget and piled into the driver's seat, slamming and locking the door quickly behind her. Josh tapped on her window.

"When can I talk to you, Marci? Will you give me your phone number so I can call you? Why are you acting so afraid of me?" he persisted. Marci looked terrified as she quickly put the car in reverse, backed out of her parking space and sped out of the parking lot.

Good grief! I didn't think she would be thrilled to see me, but I didn't expect this, either! Josh thought as he walked back to his own car, puzzled at how the judge's daughter, Marci Atwater, had reacted to him.

Linda Kay DuBose

Josh never drove through the intersection of Juniper and Franklin without glancing at the Clothing Castle, the children's apparel shop on the corner. It was fully repaired, and no one would guess by looking at it that a car had plowed through its large storefront window about seven months earlier and a young man had died there. If only hearts could be mended as quickly as buildings!

Once again Josh glanced at the shop and felt that familiar pang in his heart as he turned onto Franklin after his meeting with Mr. Murray and his strange encounter with Marci. It occurred to him that there was another young lady he should probably visit at a place he had been unable to bring himself to enter since the accident. Besides, it was lunch time, and he was hungry. Josh turned around in a parking lot and headed south on Franklin Street.

Everything looked the same in the Gator Drive-In . . . a double row of booths formed a line down the center of the room, and a single row of booths lined each of two walls. The large, open eating area was very plain in appearance. Short valances of multicolored cotton print fabric on the windows provided the only decorative touch. The smell of burgers, fries and onion rings permeated the air. Lots of teenagers and a few adults were indulging in the specialties of the house. Natalie was working hard, moving quickly from kitchen to tables and back again, taking orders and filling them. Josh seated himself in her zone and watched her as she worked. Out of the corner of her eye, she saw someone slip into the booth but did not look up to see who it was until she headed his way with a menu.

"Oh, Josh, it's you! I'm so glad to see you! How are you doing?"

"I'm doing okay, Natalie. How have you been?" Josh replied.

"I'm doing all right, Josh, but I miss my friend. I really liked Mark a lot, and I think he felt the same way about me. I know it's been tough on your family, and I pray for you every night before I go to bed."

"Thank you, Natalie. We appreciate all the prayers and the concern people have shown. This is hard for me, but I wanted to come eat at Mark's favorite place, talk to his favorite girl and make sure you're okay," Josh explained.

"That's very sweet of you, Josh. I appreciate it. Let me take your order. In just a few minutes I can go on break, and, if it's all right with you, I'd like to talk to you about something confidential." Natalie had lowered her voice and looked around to see that no one else was close enough to hear her.

"Of course, Natalie, you know you can talk to me about anything," Josh quietly responded. "Bring me Mark's favorite, please."

"One cheeseburger . . . ketchup, mustard and heavy on the pickles . . . a large order of fries and a medium Dr. Pepper . . . coming right up!" Natalie smiled.

In short order, Natalie returned with Josh's food. When she set it down before him, she slid into the booth facing him.

"I have a fifteen-minute break, Josh, and I want to tell you about something I overheard after Mark's accident and after Junior Clemons was sentenced to prison. It was early in February. I wanted to tell you before now, but, frankly, I was afraid. I didn't know if it had anything to do with Junior's case or not, but I suspected that it did, and I knew if I told what I heard I could get into trouble. The more I've thought about it, the more I knew I had to tell someone. You're easy to talk to, and I trust you not to tell anyone where you heard this. I believe your coming in today and asking about me could be a sign that God wants me to tell you this now." Natalie proceeded cautiously to reveal what she had been keeping secret.

"Junior and two of his drinking buddies used to come here occasionally to eat. About a month after Junior was sentenced, the two buddies came in one evening just before closing time. There was another guy with them that I hadn't seen before. They were the only customers here, and we had begun to clean up and get ready to close, but I took their order and gave it to the cook. Then I started wiping down all the tables. The music was playing, and they were talking quite loudly, I suppose to hear themselves above the music, and they couldn't see me over the partition between the double row of booths. It was obvious they'd been drinking and were too loose in the mouth to censor what they were saying. Their language was nasty, but I didn't dare say anything about it. I didn't know what they might do if I made them angry. Cook and I were the only ones still here, and I was just eager to get them served and out of here.

"Anyway, I was keeping my distance and working very quietly when I heard them mention Mark and Junior's car accident. Then they said something about Junior's sentencing. At that point, I moved a little nearer and started listening more closely. Junior's two buddies were laughing and telling the other person about a New Year's party they had gone to with Casey Clemons and a prank they'd pulled on a girl named Marci. It seems they drugged her and then took video of her with a cell phone. I can just imagine what kind of video it was. They said Casey, Junior's step-sister, helped them pull it off and that her dad gave them a lot of money for the phone with the video on it. I can't tell you exactly what they said, because it seemed that almost every other word was a curse word. And, I wasn't close enough to hear it all, so I can't be sure that I got the whole picture, but the bottom line is that apparently they did something bad to a girl named Marci. You know that judge who sent Junior Clemons to jail for such a short time was Judge Atwater. Well, I was curious and did a little research . . . guess what the judge's daughter's name is!"

"I don't have to guess, Natalie. It's Marci Lynn Atwater!" Josh knowingly replied, as a "light" came on.

CHAPTER 8

Josh lay in his bed that night trying to process what Natalie had told him and Marci's reaction to him at Madison's that day. Was it possible that Judge Atwater had not taken a bribe after all, but had been the victim of extortion? Could Bradley Clemons, or anyone else, actually be stupid enough to use a judge's daughter to influence his ruling? Josh had heard of jury tampering before, but never of threatening a judge or his family. Surely the judge could have that person put away with a simple phone call to the authorities, unless, of course, the extortionist had power and pull over local law enforcement.

It was no secret that Bradley Clemons had gotten away with many shady deals in the building of his financial empire. Whenever he was accused of wrongdoing, somehow the charges never did stick. Evidence was always lacking. Rumors abounded that he had "friends" in the police department. Perhaps Josh had misjudged the judge! Maybe Judge Atwater felt as helpless as Josh did when confronted with the corruption in Greystone, much of which seemed traceable to Bradley Clemons' doorstep. That corruption had never greatly concerned Josh in the past; it had not directly touched his life or his family. Now, it had become personal, affecting both his family, and the beautiful young lady whom he had admired from a distance for over a year.

Staring at the ceiling, Josh began to pour out his heart to God. He prayed for his parents and for Marci. He did not know exactly what had happened to her, but apparently something had made her very fearful, even afraid of him. It was true that Josh had lashed out at Marci's father in court, but did Marci actually believe he would take that anger out on her?

Over time, Josh's resentment toward the Clemons family had settled down to a degree, but this latest development rekindled his wrath and his determination to do all he could to expose the wickedness of Greystone's most notable tyrant and to bring him to justice. He prayed that God would show him the best way to do it.

Some six months earlier, on New Year's Day, Judge Atwater and his wife were shocked and dismayed when a taxi drove into the driveway at their home, delivering their eighteen-year-old daughter Marci from a New Year's Eve party. It was approaching three o'clock in the morning, and Marci's parents had been pacing the floor, worried sick about her. She was to have been home by one. For Marci to be late and not call home nor answer her cell phone was unheard of.

What greatly increased their stress, when the cab driver helped her to the door, was her condition. She smelled of alcohol and could not even stand up on her own. They were shocked and devastated. To their knowledge, Marci had never before consumed a drop of alcoholic beverage of any type, and now she had come home in the wee hours of the morning, fall-down drunk! Sitting in the dark taxi, unseen by the Atwaters, Casey Clemons watched as Marci was safely assisted into the arms of her anxious parents by the kindhearted cab driver.

Marci's mom had undressed her and helped her into bed. As their daughter slept soundly, her parents remained sleepless. At eight o'clock that morning, their phone rang.

"Good morning, Judge, and Happy New Year to you and all your beautiful family!" Bradley Clemons' syrupy voice oozed a sticky greeting. "I'm just calling to see if Marci made it home okay last night, or this morning I should say. I've been really concerned about her since my step-daughter Casey came home and told me what happened at the party."

"Marci's home and she's fine, Bradley. Thank you for your concern. You have a good day," Judge Atwater replied guardedly and abruptly cut the conversation short. He did not care to hear what Bradley Clemons had to say. He preferred to get his information from Marci when she awoke.

"Well, now, don't be in such a hurry, Judge," Clemons doggedly continued. "There's something you should know. I'm sure it'll be unpleasant to hear . . . none of us like to get bad news about our children, but I think it's my duty to inform you of the situation that occurred last night.

"Casey said that Marci did some major drinking at the party and got drunker than a sailor on leave. The host family wasn't serving the liquor, of course, but there was plenty being secretly passed around, according to Casey. Some of the young folks did as they often do at parties like that. They slipped in their own liquor. I suppose it became somewhat of a game to see if they could get away with it. Of course, Marci's under the legal drinking age, but with so many others indulging, it must have been too hard for her to resist. Kids will be kids, you know!"

Running out of patience, the judge interrupted Bradley's ramblings. "Mr. Clemons, if you have a point to make, please get to it."

"Just be patient, Judge. I definitely have a point to make, and I'm getting there. Anyway, your daughter wound up in an upstairs bedroom with a couple of fellows, and Casey walked in on them just in time. Marci had, shall we say . . . 'disrobed' and was putting on quite a steamy performance for the guys. One of the fellows was making a video of her with his cell phone camera. Goodness knows what else may have happened if Casey hadn't arrived when she did and put a stop to it. She demanded the phone from the boy and brought it home with her. It was one of those disposable type phones, so I don't figure he'll be trying to get it back, knowing it could get him in a lot of trouble.

"Just think! If Casey hadn't gotten that phone when she did, that video could have been circulated all around town and perhaps even found its way to the Internet. You needn't worry, though. I have the cell phone, and I'll just hang on to it for safe keeping. I want you to know that, out of respect for you and your family, I have not viewed the video and have no intention of looking at it. I don't think I could bear to see your sweet little girl carrying on like that. I'm sure she would never do such things when she's sober. Alcohol has caused my son to do some things he would never ordinarily do too; so you can be sure I understand your situation, Judge."

"Okay, Clemons, where are you going with this? I know you well enough to know you don't really care what happens to my daughter," the judge interjected. "If you cared, you'd simply delete the video, and that would be that. But I'm sure you have something else in mind, so out with it!"

"Aw now, Judge, you're misjudging me! Of course I care deeply about Marci, and you, and your wife and your whole family. In time, I expect I'll delete it, but let's not be hasty. It could be evidence if you ever needed it for any reason. But it does upset me to think what an embarrassment it would be for all of you if that video ever got out . . . you being a Baptist deacon and all that, much less a judge. But, you know, that's just how it is with us parents; we like to help other parents look out for their kids when they make a mistake, if you know what I mean. I'm sure you'd do the same for me. Isn't that right?" Clemons' serpentine insinuations slithered through the phone line, his meaning emerging clearly.

"Clemons, you're a disgrace! How dare you threaten me and try to influence my ruling on your son's case? You should know me well enough to know that I can't be bought, and I will not break the law for you or anyone else! I will recuse myself from the case before I'll let you influence me or hurt my daughter. I'll call the police and have you arrested for extortion!" The judge, red-faced with anger, fired back at Clemons.

"Well, now, Judge. You're getting all upset over nothing. I'm not trying to influence anything, and I'm certainly not asking you to break any laws. I know what the penalty for my son's actions could be, and I know you have a lot of latitude in determining how severe a sentence he gets. Naturally, as his father, I'd like to see Junior get the lightest possible sentence within the limits of the law, but have you heard me make any kind of threat? Why, no indeed! You're imagining things, Judge. We're simply two fathers with kids who have made some bad decisions, and we can sympathize with each other, don't you think? Look at it this way. My son made a mistake in judgement. What he did cannot be deleted, but his consequences can be minimized. Why should your daughter's mistakes be deleted? Shouldn't she have to face some consequences too?

"Junior is acting in good faith by pleading 'no contest'. I'm proud of him for that, and no matter what the sentence is I'm going to do my best to keep a tight lid on that nasty little video. Of course, you understand, I can't guarantee anything, but I'll work as hard as you do to keep all this ugly business with Marci minimized. That's an interesting word, isn't it . . . ? *Minimized!* Yes, I like that word! Don't you?"

"Bradley Clemons, you're a snake in the grass! How do I know this is not a total fabrication? Just because you say there's a video doesn't prove there is one."

"Really now, Judge! Are you calling me a liar? Here I am trying to help your daughter, and you talk to me like that? Let me assure you there were at least three witnesses, including Casey, maybe more. But the best way to find out is to ask your own daughter. She'll know . . . that is, if she wasn't too drunk to remember!

"Now, if you think this conversation was out of order and you want to call the police, let me save you the trouble. My good buddy, the Chief of Police, is standing right here, as a witness to this call. If you want to make a complaint to him, you certainly may, but I'm afraid he's just not going to agree that I've said or done anything amiss. How about it, do you want to speak to him?" Clemons grinned at the chief when the next sound he heard was a dial tone.

CHAPTER 9

The Clemons family had never been what anyone could consider a happy, wholesome household except, perhaps, during those early years when Bradley was married to his first wife, Kate, and he was just starting out in business. The couple didn't have much money, but they were deeply in love, and Bradley was determined to become a millionaire by the time he was thirty-five and a multi-millionaire after that. It was his singular goal in life.

Bradley had been brought up in a very poor family in a run-down trailer park on the wrong side of the tracks. It was one of those areas where old, beat-up, rusted-out automobiles, washing machines, refrigerators and such cluttered some of the yards, and where aluminum foil served as window shades to keep out the hot sunlight. Sadly, his neighborhood was often referred to as the "trashy trailer park on Tanner Road." As a youth, he had hated his life and bitterly watched the "upper-crust" kids in school wear their nice clothes, eat their fine food, drive their new cars and live in their large, elaborate homes. Starting with practically nothing but dogged determination and excessive ambition, Bradley set out to build his wealth, by hook or by crook. In fact, he became obsessed with greed.

After three years of marriage, Bradley's compulsion to work long hours and to put every cent possible back into his business was beginning to create a strain on the marriage relationship. However, when Kate announced that she was pregnant, Bradley was overjoyed. Kate had a difficult pregnancy, suffering toxemia brought on by pregnancy-induced hypertension, but little Bradley Jr. almost made it to full term and was delivered safely. However, Kate oddly continued to battle high blood pressure and was on medication to control it. When Little Bradley was only three months old, Kate suffered a mild stroke. It was followed by another severe stroke three weeks later, from which she did not recover. Just days later, she died. The bitterness raging inside Bradley mushroomed exponentially. His tiny son and his financial ambition became the total substance of his world.

****

Janice had known from the beginning of her marriage to Bradley that he didn't love her with the same kind of love she had for him. She had been a friend to Kate, and Bradley turned to her for help with the baby after Kate's death. Janice was recently divorced and had a small child of her own, a little girl named Casey. Casey's dad had forsaken her and her mom, having left them for another woman.

Bradley hired Janice to take care of Junior while he was at work, and Junior bonded with Janice almost as if she were his mother. Casey was like a big sister. Two years after Kate's death, Bradley proposed to Janice, and she accepted. Janice had fallen in love with Bradley, but for him this was strictly a marriage of convenience. Janice had harbored high hopes that in time she would be able to win Bradley's heart, and she tried very hard to please him in every way.

Now, after almost twenty years of a mock marriage, Janice clearly understood what a poor proposition the arrangement had been for her. Oh, yes, she had financial security, high social standing, and a comfortable home for herself and her daughter. She actually loved Junior as if he were her own son, and Casey loved him too. But Bradley's indifference toward Janice had steadily morphed into contempt, and he treated her shamefully. The love Janice had once felt for Bradley changed as well. It had been shattered by disappointment, dread and fear.

She would have left him years earlier, but for three things. First, she could not totally extinguish that small ember of hope that Bradley would change and their marriage could improve. Second, Junior needed a mother, and Casey needed a father. Third, her self-confidence was so depleted she did not believe she could survive on her own. Besides, she knew Bradley would not allow her to leave . . . . not because he loved her and would miss her, but because it would wound his ego for others to observe the failure of his marriage. Bradley Clemons didn't fail to get, or to keep, whatever he wanted! Janice also knew that a major reason Bradley had not divorced her was that he was not willing to divide his "worldly goods" with her. Divorce would be entirely too expensive for Bradley! And now, having received her doctor's latest report, Janice was in a seemingly hopeless and dire situation.

Junior's one-year prison sentence was now approximately half-way served. During Junior's absence, Bradley had been even more difficult to live with. The anonymous notes he continued to receive weekly did nothing to sweeten his disposition. Another jail cell drawing had arrived in today's mail.

"What in @#$%'s wrong with you, woman?" Bradley barked from his end of the massive, formal dining table when Janice's glass slipped from her hand and tumbled over on the table. "You're getting as clumsy as an ox. Is it too much to ask that you not spill things at the table like a three-year-old?"

Janice was seated at the opposite end of the impressive table, and Casey sat on one side. Casey faced an empty chair across from her and an unused, full place setting of china, silverware, and crystal where Junior should have been seated. On the three nights each week that Bradley insisted the family dine together formally, the servants were required to set the table for four, regardless of Junior's absence.

In addition, the cook, Lucy, was instructed to remain in the kitchen while the butler, wearing a formal suit complete with jacket and bow tie, served the food very methodically. When the meal was ready and the family seated, Luke, the butler, would announce very ceremoniously, "**Dinner is served**," and the charade would begin. Bradley had an exaggerated notion of how the wealthy dine at home, probably a carryover from old movies. As ridiculous as it seemed to the rest of the household, they indulged him the exercise in faux aristocracy because he demanded it and because it seemed to stroke his ego. How the family dined the other four nights of the week mattered little to Bradley for he was seldom there.

"I'm sorry, Bradley. I don't know how that happened. I guess I'm just a little nervous tonight," Janice meekly apologized. "I received some disturbing test results from the doctor today. He said...."

"Oh, save it, Janice!" Bradley angrily interrupted. "All you do is run to doctors and whine and complain about how you feel. I've spent a small fortune on doctors for you just in the last year, and I'm fed up with it. Here's a diagnosis for you, 'you're a hypochondriac!' Just shut up and let me eat one meal in peace without hearing about all your petty ailments!"

Casey knew better than to say a word. She simply got up immediately when the glass of tea was spilled and began to clean it up. Luke quickly took over the task and assured Janice that it was no problem at all. Casey glanced sympathetically at her mother and wished she could slap her stepfather's arrogant jaw! But, she too lived in dread and fear of Bradley Clemons. He controlled Casey the same way he did Janice, through intimidation, and both women felt helpless to escape his tyrannical grip on their lives. At least Casey had more freedom to stay away from home and avoid his ill temper than her mother did. But the latest thing Bradley had forced Casey to do was still troubling her. Marci was a good girl and had been very kind to Casey. Why did she not have the backbone to refuse being a part of such an ugly plot against Marci, and what could she do about it now?

****

Amyotrophic Lateral Sclerosis, ALS! The doctor's report confirms that I have it. But I don't even have the luxury of sharing that horrible news with a loving, concerned husband! Is there a punier, more pathetic person in this world than the wealthy Mrs. Bradley Clemons Sr.? Janice reflected sardonically as she lay alone in her plush, king-sized, four-poster bed that night, crying. None of the elaborate, expensive furnishings surrounding her offered the slightest bit of consolation.

Linda Kay DuBose

I could tell Casey, and she would care, but how can I burden her down with one more problem? I'm actually glad Bradley stopped me from telling it at supper tonight. It was the wrong time and the wrong place. I had not intended to tell them at that moment. It was the spilled tea and Bradley's scolding that brought the words to my lips. I know now that it's got to be my secret for a little while longer. My life's been a living hell for a very long time, and I've dragged Casey through it with me. Oh, how I messed up when I tried to step into Kate's shoes all those years ago! Bradley doesn't love me . . . never has. He's had one affair after another, and I've had to live with it. He's as mean as a snake, and I can hardly stand to hear his voice or see his face another day. I know what's ahead for me. ALS will do to me what it did to Lou Gehrig. But before it does, I'll see to it that when I'm gone, Casey will be free of the evil Mr. Bradley Clemons!

CHAPTER 10

"I don't know why you waste your time reading that fairytale book," Junior scoffed. It was not the first time he had ridiculed his cellmate, Richard Levitt, for reading his Bible. "You think somehow you're gonna' get a special miracle, and the doors'll just open up, and you'll waltz right out of here . . . rescued by some 'SUPERMAN' in the sky?"

Junior continued to poke fun at Richard. "I think everybody that believes that stupid book ought to be locked up and the key thrown away. That religious stuff is for weaklings who don't know how to get what they want on their own. They just shut their eyes, ask for what they want, and when it doesn't happen they accept it as 'Gooooood's wiiiiiiill'!" Junior mocked as he dramatically and sarcastically elongated the last two words. "I've seen how it works, and I'm not fooled by any of it. If I were you, I'd throw that book away and get myself a *Playboy Magazine*. Now that's what I call good reading!" Junior laughed contemptuously at Richard.

Richard patiently looked up at Junior, determined not to let him get under his skin. The things Junior said were typical of the other "lost" inmates with whom he'd tried to share his faith. They put up their best defense against the gospel by being as offensive as they could be. Richard believed that, deep down, most of them just wanted someone to be brave enough and wise enough to convince them they were wrong because, as they were, they had little hope in this life and none for the life to come.

"No, my friend, I don't expect to be miraculously set free from this prison. However, it did happen to some other fellows back in Bible days when they were spreading the gospel and some folks that felt the same way about that as you do had them thrown in prison. It happened to Peter and, on another occasion, to Paul and Silas. You see, they didn't belong in prison, but I do. They were just being preachers like God wanted them to be. I lost my temper and killed my wife. I've no right to ask God to set me free," Richard replied calmly.

Junior was silenced by Richard's candor. He'd heard rumors that Richard had murdered his wife, but dared not ask him about it.

Richard continued, "You see, I was already a Christian, but I wasn't a good one. I became a believer when I was a kid, growing up in the church. But when I went off to college, I sort of put God way up on a shelf where I couldn't see Him, and just started to live it up with my pals. I did things I never believed I'd do, and I got further and further from the teachings in this book and what my mom and dad had taught me. I wanted to do things **my** way and have a good time.

"Eventually, I graduated and got married. I didn't choose a godly girl to marry, but one who enjoyed partying as much as I did. However, I didn't bargain on her 'partying' with my best friend while I was at work. I came home early one day and found them together in our bed. I totally lost control, pulled my wife off the bed and slung her across the room. She fell awkwardly against the corner of the dresser, and it broke her neck. So, she's dead, and I'm here!"

"Well, you don't seem to be too bothered about being here. I'm climbing the walls, about to go nuts.

You're as cool as a cucumber. Don't you want to get out of this place?"

"Of course I want to get out of here! I want my freedom as much as you do. But here's the thing . . . I've already gotten another kind of freedom that you don't have. I got forgiveness; so, even though I still deeply regret what I did, I don't drag my guilt around like a ball and chain anymore. I asked God to forgive me for killing my wife and for having disobeyed Him all those years that led up to my big collision with destiny. I chose the wrong path, and the wrong path always leads to the wrong place. I'm through trying to live my life without God's help. I've learned how easy it is to get all messed up. From now on, no matter where I am, I'm going to let Him lead me, and I'll follow just as closely as I can. I won't be in this place forever, but while I'm here, I'm going to share with the rest of you guys what Jesus has done for me. What you do with that is up to you!"

Richard returned to reading his Bible while Junior sat quietly on the side of his bunk, pondering what he had just heard. It all sounded foreign, but he never doubted for a moment that Richard was sincere. Junior would have to learn more about this way of life Richard talked about before he could decide if it was for him. However, there was one point on which Junior could already agree with Richard . . . *when you choose the wrong path, you end up in the wrong place.* He might could even muster up an "amen" to that!

****

Another letter arrived from that preacher addressed to Bradley Clemons Jr. The guard put it away with the others. He had strict orders from Junior's father (and a nice little stipend, as well) for screening Junior's in-coming and out-going mail. Junior knew too much about all the Clemons "enterprises" to be softened by any preacher's sweet talk. Bradley didn't like at all what that religious fanatic had said at the sentencing, and he wasn't going to give him a chance to work on Junior by mail. A religious conversion could be the ruination of Bradley and all his cronies. Therefore, no letters or visits to Junior would be allowed from anyone named *Williams*.

CHAPTER 11

Just exactly what was Clemons Enterprises all about, anyway? Actually, just a few trusted "partners in crime" knew the answer to that question, and they, only partially. Bradley Clemons was the solitary one who knew the full extent of his profit-making activities, but he couldn't successfully engineer them all without the participation, patronage and protection of certain others. One of the secrets of his success was actually to practice something vaguely biblical . . . not letting the left hand know what the right hand is doing. However, Clemons was not giving to the needy, as was the context of that biblical advice. No, he was taking away with both hands as much and as often as he could, hoping to keep it all secret. But, as the rest of that passage could have warned him, the Father above was seeing it all.

One part of his business portfolio that was legitimate, to an extent, was the front behind which he operated his shadiest dealings. That was the initial business he had started when he was married to his first wife, Kate. He began a small industrial garment manufacturing company in Greystone, producing work uniforms, and named it Clemons Industrial Garment Manufacturing Plant. He began with only a dozen employees and a handful of sewing machines, cutting tables, and steam presses.

Bradley had lived for three years with his grandparents in another state after finishing high school and had worked on the production line in such a factory. He liked the work, learned all he could about every aspect of it, and saw the potential to start his own plant back home. With all he could borrow from the bank plus a loan from his grandparents added to his own savings, he started on a very small scale. With lots of hard work, the business took off and grew steadily until he needed more room to expand the plant. That's when things got sticky. Other businesses surrounding his didn't want to give up their space. Clemons, not willing to look for another location on which to rebuild, gradually, through intimidation and other under-handed methods, drove the other businesses away, and Clemons Industrial Garment Manufacturing Plant now sprawled out over the entire square block.

Many good people made a decent (but not overly-generous) wage working in the garment factory from eight a.m. to four p.m. five days a week. But what went on in parts of the expansive plant on certain nights was neither decent nor lawful. Whenever casual observers saw a group of men and women dressed in work clothes entering the building for the evening shift, they assumed they were the skeleton crew that took care of maintenance and continued production, along with packing and shipping processes, carried out on a limited scale at night. They were only partially correct. There was more going on than met the eye.

Not only did Bradley Clemons own the garment plant and use it for other profitable (and illegal) operations, he had bought out or created several other businesses in Greystone. He owned a bakery, a restaurant, a dry-cleaning establishment, and an automobile repair/body shop. Under the umbrella organization called "Clemons Enterprises," Bradley employed one main accountant to manage the bookkeeping matters concerning those four businesses, and she had special abilities when it came to hiding profits, fabricating expenses, and skimming funds off the top so that Clemons' tax bills could be reduced. That, and more, endeared her to Bradley.

The striking redhead, Taressa Tomlinson, was one beauty of a bookkeeper and had, from the beginning, set her sights on Bradley. Her low-cut blouses and high-hemmed skirts, coupled with flirtation and flattery, went a long way in helping her to capture her prey. But the adulterous relationship between them was showing signs of wear.

Bradley had been promising to divorce Janice and marry Taressa for nearly five years, and it just wasn't happening. Not only that, their secret rendezvous were fewer and farther between these days, and they almost always ended in an argument of some sort. Taressa was quite sure someone else had caught Bradley's eye, and it was only a matter of time before Taressa would be "a fling of the past!" She would not go quietly . . . nor empty-handed!

CHAPTER 12

*B*radley Clemons was not the only person who had friends in law enforcement. It just so happened that Judge Atwater had a very close friend who worked for the FBI. As soon as the judge had talked with Marci about the New Year's Eve party, it was clear to him that she had not been drunk, but had been drugged. Marci could remember nothing with clarity beyond drinking a ginger ale and getting very lightheaded, feeling as though she might faint. She vaguely recalled someone helping her up the stairs and saying that she didn't look well and should lie down for a while. She thought it was Casey Clemons, but couldn't say for sure.

Marci could neither confirm nor deny what Bradley Clemons had said about her and the two boys because she had no memory of the hours that had elapsed between going up the stairs at the party and waking up in her own bed near noon the next day. She was terrified to think about what might have taken place while she was defenseless.

It was the second day of January. Judge Atwater was scheduled to rule on Junior Clemons' sentencing on January 4th. The judge picked up the phone and called Noah Crenshaw, his friend in the FBI.

"Noah, I'm in a mess. I need some off-the-record, confidential advice right away. I need to get a scoundrel put behind bars without ruining my daughter's reputation and my own career. When and where can you meet me? I don't want to say any more over the phone," the judge entreated his friend.

The following day at noon, the two men met at Dora's Diner in Midvale, forty miles from Greystone, and Judge Atwater shared the details of the extortion Bradley Clemons was attempting to perpetrate against him.

"Noah, I've got to make a ruling on Junior Clemons' sentencing tomorrow, so I don't have much time to figure this out. I need some help immediately. I can't go to the local police because there's no doubt the Chief of Police is as crooked as a country road and quite possibly some of the officers on the force as well. I've got to bypass them to get help with this problem."

After receiving a detailed account of the judge's dilemma, Noah Crenshaw proposed a plan. "Nathan, we need to get this guy and put him away for a very long time. But, as it stands, it's your word against his. You have no proof that your conversation with him ever took place. He's a shrewd operator. As a matter of fact, we've known him by reputation and have kept him on our radar for a quite a while. But he really knows how to get what he wants and cover his tracks in the process. So far, we haven't been able to put together a strong enough case against him to reasonably ensure a conviction if we pressed charges. We need to get one step ahead of him and give him enough rope to hang himself. I think I know how we can do that.

"I suggest you lead him to believe that he has you right where he wants you. Go ahead and deliver the minimum one-year sentence tomorrow. We can deal with the ramifications of that later, and we need time to get my plan laid out. At least his out-of-control son will be off the streets, and later we can work on extending his stay. When the sentencing session is over, we'll stage a little scheme of our own. This time, you'll have the leverage.

"I want you to call him from your home phone, which we will have tapped, and tell him that you suddenly have a renewed interest concerning additional charges that were brought against Junior in the past. Tell him that you intend to see to it Junior comes to court again to face those charges unless Clemons turns that video over to you or shows you evidence that it has been deleted and not forwarded to any other device.

"Clemons is all too aware that his son has prior arrests and charges that were swept under the rug. He also knows you have the power to get those charges resurrected, reinvestigated, and brought to trial. Threaten to get the State and Federal Bureaus of Investigation to delve into past allegations against Bradley, too. There's a whole list of them. That should get his attention! I can certainly supply you with enough information to put the fear of God in him. You can ask him if that video is worth a long prison sentence for his son and an even longer one for him.

"Of course, he may call your bluff, and there's little chance that he can actually give you assurance that the video is not stored somewhere else. But what we're after is not primarily the cell phone video. What we really need is for him to stick his foot in his mouth. If he says anything that indicates he tried to intimidate you into giving a biased ruling, we'll have him dead to rights. It may or may not work, but it's worth a try.

"Unfortunately, it wouldn't completely relieve your angst about that video's getting out. I don't know that there's much we can do about that. Just one click of a button and it's out there, never to be reeled back in. But if you're successful at getting him to say something incriminating, we'd finally have all we need to put this guy away, and that would make your town, if not the whole state, a much better place for decent folks to live! I know I'm asking you to do something unorthodox, but what have you got to lose? Will you do it?"

****

The whole scheme sounded a bit dramatic to Judge Atwater, but, without a better idea, he agreed to follow Noah Crenshaw's advice and to go along with his plan. Two days after Junior's sentencing, the FBI had the phones tapped at the Atwater home. The technicians had come in under the guise of plumbers, driving a plumber's van. They worked quickly and efficiently and then left. Nathan Atwater had waited anxiously for the appointed time to make the call, eight o'clock in the evening, two days after Junior's sentencing.

"Clemons, this is Nathan Atwater. I'm not going to waste words with you about this. I'm calling to tell you that I've done what you wanted, and now I want that phone with the video of my daughter on it. If you think I'm going to allow you to hold on to that and use it against me in the future, you can forget it. I accommodated you once, but that's it! You name the time and place, but I want that thing in my hands tomorrow and not one day later! Do you understand?" The judge emphatically made his demands clear and waited with bated breath to see if Clemons would say the right words.

"Well, good evening, Judge. It's nice to hear from you. I want to thank you for showing compassion for Junior. My wife and I are forever indebted to you for looking on our son with merciful eyes. I must say I was pleasantly surprised, and I hope this year will be a time of reflection and growing up for Junior. Granted, you could have done even better on his behalf . . . you know, first offender status with all probation, but I understand that may have been too hard for some folks to accept. One year behind bars is not so bad. Maybe this is just what Junior needs to make him a little more serious about life.

"But what's this about a phone and a video? I don't know what you mean? Could you explain that to me?" Clemons poured on his syrupy sarcasm once again. And, true to form, he expertly covered his tracks.

Giving it his best effort, Nathan plowed forward. "Don't give me that bull, Clemons! You know exactly what I'm talking about! You threatened to broadcast that terrible video of my daughter at the New Year's party if I didn't go easy on Junior. And, by the way, Marci was not drunk; she was drugged. She's not responsible for anything on that video. Our doctor is running tests to find out what substance was used to incapacitate her. And you can be sure that sooner or later I'll find out who drugged her, too.

"Meanwhile, I have no intention of letting you hold that video over my head again. Just know this . . . I have some powerful weapons in my arsenal, too. How would you like for me to reopen investigations into some of Junior's past run-ins with the law that got swept under the rug? And how would you like it if I went to the State Police or the FBI and had them check into the devious ways you acquired the land for your plant? And how would you like it if I tipped off the IRS that you need to be investigated for tax evasion? I'm not playing around with you Clemons. I've thought a lot about it. If I don't get some assurances that I can stop worrying about that video, I'm going to give you a lot to worry about. Do you understand?"

Judge Atwater again waited anxiously. Surely Clemons would have to respond in such a way as to prove himself guilty of extortion. But the wily Clemons was on his toes tonight.

"Judge, I don't have the foggiest idea what you're talking about or why you're threatening me with such absurdities. I don't know anything about a video or any drugs, and I certainly have never threatened you about anything! Where on earth did you get that notion? Yes, I have heard reports that Marci was drinking heavily the night of the party, but far be it from me to ever spread such rumors or try to use that information in some underhanded way. Actually, I'm quite offended that you're accusing me of such a thing.

"Maybe you need to take a reality check. Are you sure your daughter's telling you the truth? I hate to say it, but it could be she's claiming she was drugged to avoid your disapproval. And if there were drugs in her system, maybe it's because she was experimenting with drugs, voluntarily. Test results couldn't answer that question, could they?"

The judge's blood pressure was soaring, but he remained silent, allowing Bradley to continue uninterrupted.

"It seems to me, sir, that you're under stress dealing with a teenager who's going through some growing pains. Believe me, I understand your predicament. I hope things turn around for Marci before she gets into more serious trouble. Take it from a parent who's been in your shoes. You just can't ever tell what young people are up to. You have to keep a very close eye on them. I wish you well, Judge. Good night!"

****

Months passed. The video issue seemingly could not be resolved. Marci tried to put it out of her mind. She managed to complete the last semester of the school year, but she couldn't entirely shake the fact that she may have unknowingly behaved in a most ungodly manner and that any day now the world could become a witness to it.

How would she ever be able to hold her head up in public if that vulgar video were to surface? Her reputation would be destroyed, and it could very well affect her ability to serve in her church or to get a respectable, high-level job in the future. It would be a very ugly skeleton in her closet that would be difficult to keep there. Would any young man with high moral standards want to date her, much less take her home to meet his mom? Would she become a locker room joke to the other kind of guys, and would they hound her for dates? Could some people already know about the video and be whispering behind her back? It was all very unsettling.

Marci's parents decided not to push for an investigation into the incident because if they did, gossip about Marci's being drunk or drugged and an alleged vulgar video would surely begin to circulate, even if the video itself never did. People would probably imagine the worst. The possibility the Atwaters had feared the most was that Marci might have been raped, but, thankfully, there was no physical evidence of that. The urine test results showed traces of a type of "party" drug that could be classified as a date-rape drug. But, as Clemons had hinted, it would be difficult to prove she had not taken it willingly. Marci had no idea who slipped her the drug, so there was no one to charge with the crime.

Mr. and Mrs. Atwater felt it was better to keep the whole incident quiet. If the video ever did come out, they would deal with it then. But, as long as Bradley Clemons remained silent about it, they could too. Clemons had had no occasion as yet to attempt to hold the video over the judge's head again. Hopefully, he never would.

Casey Clemons held another piece of the confusing puzzle concerning what had happened the night of the party. According to Bradley, Casey claimed that Marci had been drinking so heavily that she was totally drunk, which was entirely false. Marci also vaguely remembered Casey helping her up the stairs to lie down. And then there was the fact that Casey wound up with the phone containing the video and turned it over to Bradley. That could mean only one thing; Casey had been a part of Bradley's plan, but there was no way to prove it. If only Marci could remember, but the drug had made that impossible.

Marci had wanted to confront Casey, but her parents advised against it. "Let sleeping dogs lie," they said. "If she was involved, she would never admit it for fear of going to jail. She would simply echo her stepfather's account of the situation." It was obvious to the Atwaters that Bradley and Janice Clemons had reared two lawless children, both of whom should be locked away along with Bradley.

Although there was no indication that Janice Clemons had been directly involved, it was quite possible that she, too, was complicit in the matter. Casey had graduated and was no longer at Easterling College. Marci had not seen her since the party. Perhaps it was for the best.

Marci had avoided Josh at school the last semester. She felt awkward knowing that he was angry with her dad and probably doubted his integrity. She couldn't blame him, but she couldn't justify her father's decision to him either, not without disclosing the fact that she had a "dirty little secret." Josh was the last person on earth that Marci wanted to know about the troublesome video. They had only been casual friends. They'd never even had a date, but she felt sad that there was a wall between them now. Their families were at odds, and she couldn't tell him why.

CHAPTER 13

The summer had ended, the first summer after Mark's death, the summer Josh had spent working with Cameron Lawn Service. Another year of classes at Eastering College was about to begin for both Josh Williams and Marci Atwater. On a warm mid-August evening, the phone rang at the Atwater home.

"Good evening, Judge Atwater. My name is Josh Williams. I'm sorry to call you at home, but I need to talk to you privately about a personal matter. First, though, I need to apologize for shouting at you when you sentenced Junior Clemons to only one year in prison back in January. I'm sure you remember that morning as well as I do. It was a very difficult day for me, my parents, and all our friends, but I think I misjudged you.

"I thought you were a friend of Bradley Clemons or that perhaps he had paid you to go easy on his son, but I know better than that now. I hope you'll forgive me for jumping to the wrong conclusion. That's what I want to talk to you about, that and what I've learned Bradley Clemons did . . . something that is very disturbing to me." Josh hurriedly spilled out his well-rehearsed speech in hopes that he could finish it before the judge hung up on him. The judge was surprised to be getting a call from Josh and remained silent for a few moments, letting the whole monologue sink in. Josh thought perhaps he had, indeed, hung up the phone.

"Hello? Judge, are you there?"

"Oh, yes, I'm here, Josh. I'm just a little surprised to be hearing from you. Tell me something, young man, what makes you think that you misjudged me? What have you learned that changed your mind?"

"Well, Judge, I don't really want to talk in specifics about that over the phone, but I will tell you that I'm acquainted with your daughter Marci from college. I think she's a really nice girl, and, to be honest, I've been trying to scrape up the courage to ask her out on a date, but she avoided me like the plague all last semester. And recently, when I saw her at the music store, she practically ran away from me. I think what I have to tell her may clear the air between us and also relieve her of any worry she may have about a certain party she attended last New Year's Eve. Would you allow me to come to your house or meet you someplace where we could talk privately as soon as possible?"

"Young man, I'm certainly interested in having that conversation with you. We're just about to sit down to supper, but if you could be here in about an hour, I'll see you this evening. Will that work for you?"

"That's perfect. Thank you very much. I'll be there at eight o'clock. Oh, and may I bring my dad and a friend who really needs to come with us?"

"Yes, of course. I look forward to meeting with the three of you."

"Good! We'll see you in a little while." Josh hung up the phone in his dad's church office and turned to share the plan with his dad and his friend. Pastor Williams was seated at his desk, and the two young people were seated in the chairs on the opposite side of the desk. The three of them were on a mission, and this part of it could not have worked out better. They would not have to wait another day

Greystone Hearts

to put this matter of Marci and the video to rest. The threesome talked a while longer and then spent some time in prayer before getting into the pastor's car and driving to their appointment with Judge Atwater.

Meanwhile, Nathan Atwater was barely able to eat his supper. He wondered if he should ask his wife and daughter to be present for the meeting with Josh, his dad, and the unidentified friend. But, because of the uncertainty surrounding the matter and the involvement of the FBI, he decided that he should hear Josh's story first, before he could decide who else in the family should hear it.

Leaving his plate of food only half eaten, the judge excused himself from the table and went to freshen up before his guests arrived. Then he seated himself at the desk in his home office. The judge bowed his head and asked God to give him wisdom in dealing with the situation at hand. He prayed that what he was about to hear would not make Marci's predicament, and his, any worse. If Josh was being straightforward, perhaps this meeting was going to be a positive experience.

"Lord, I could use a little good news tonight. Please, let it be so!" The judge prayed and waited.

Marci was asked to remain upstairs while her dad had a confidential meeting with some guests in his office. Her brother, one year younger, was spending the night at a friend's house. The two youngest children, ten and twelve, selected a movie on DVD to watch in the den. Marci's mom, Betty, busied herself in the kitchen, cleaning up after the evening meal.

Nathan answered the doorbell, led the three visitors into his study, and closed the door. He doubted that he had successfully concealed his surprise when he realized that the third person, "the friend who needed to come with them," was none other than Casey Clemons.

CHAPTER 14

Following the preliminary niceties, Pastor Williams took the lead in getting down to business. "Judge Atwater, while Josh and Casey were both attending Easterling College, before Casey graduated last year, they became casual friends. When all this happened with Mark's death and Junior's being sent to prison, Casey was caught in a difficult position. She began to do some serious thinking about her own life and that of her family. Recently, she decided to call Josh and talk to him about everything that had happened and about the turmoil she felt in her heart. Josh persuaded her to come to me for spiritual counseling. I'm very happy to say that in those meetings Casey came to see that her greatest need was to have a personal relationship with Jesus Christ. She has become a believer in Him and has started a new life. I know that you're a Christian too, and a deacon in your church, so I'm certain you can appreciate the importance of that commitment and can rejoice with us about it."

"Absolutely!" the judge responded with genuine enthusiasm. "That's wonderful news, Casey, and I'm very happy to hear it!"

"Well, Casey also made another decision," the minister continued. "She wants to tell you about that in her own words. We put no pressure on her to do this; it's entirely her choice. She asked Josh and me to come with her for moral support, and we were happy to do it. It took a lot of courage for her to come here and face you with her story, but we hope you will listen with an open mind and a soft heart. Start when you're ready, Casey. The floor is all yours." All eyes turned to the young woman who sat nervously with her head bowed and her hands clenched tightly together in her lap. Casey hesitated, finding it difficult to know how to start.

Josh, sensitive to her reluctance and discomfort, reached out and placed his hand on her shoulder in a gesture of encouragement. "It's okay, Casey, don't be afraid. You're going to feel much better when you get this burden off your shoulders, and nobody here is going to jump on your case. Just start from the beginning and tell the judge what you told my dad and me."

Casey began to slowly and carefully tell her story. "Judge Atwater, as you probably know, Bradley Clemons is my stepfather. He's a very difficult a man to live with, but I still care about him because he's the only dad I've ever known. There are times when I feel like I hate him, but then I think about how he's provided for me and my mother all these years and how he used to be more kind than he has been in recent years. I feel a certain loyalty to him, but that loyalty has been stretched to the breaking point. I've learned the hard way that a false sense of obligation can cause people to do bad things, things that hurt innocent people." Casey paused to take a deep breath and then continued.

"Over the years I've watched Bradley turn a sweet little boy, my stepbrother Junior, into a spoiled brat, then into a headstrong teenager, and eventually into an irresponsible alcoholic. I love my stepbrother dearly, but I was powerless to do anything about his downward spiral.

"Another thing that was happening before my eyes, and that I could not prevent, was the destruction of my mother's dignity. My mother was once a happy, out-going, vivacious lady. Bradley slowly whittled away at those characteristics over the years and has turned her into a virtual invalid, emotionally, especially when she's in his presence.

"After Mark was killed in the automobile accident and you were scheduled to determine Junior's sentence, my stepfather demanded that I help him with a scheme he was planning. He thought he could make you willing to give Junior a very short prison term, or maybe only probation. He told me that if I didn't participate I was turning my back on Junior and that it would be my fault if he had to stay in prison for several years. I wanted no part of it, but he was so angry and insistent that I gave in and helped to put the plan in motion.

"A friend of mine who knows Marci happened to mention that Marci was planning to be at the same New Year's party I would be attending. At the dinner table a couple of nights before the party, I made the mistake of naming some of the people I knew who would be at the party. Marci was one of those I named, and Bradley seized on it. He decided that would be the perfect opportunity to get something on Marci that he could use for Junior's benefit.

"He made arrangements for a couple of Junior's friends to escort me to the party. Once we arrived, they milled around in the crowd and kept an eye on Marci, waiting for the perfect opportunity to do what Bradley hired them to do. One of the guys slipped a drug into her ginger ale when she left it on a table and walked away for a few minutes. When she came back and finished her drink, she began to get very sleepy and dizzy. The two guys and I helped her up the stairs as discreetly as possible.

"It was a huge house, and we took her to one of the remote guest bedrooms where we didn't expect to be found. We placed her on the bed, and locked the bedroom door. The whole thing was only supposed to take a few minutes, and then we'd leave her asleep on the bed." Casey stopped for another deep breath. The next part of the story was the hardest part to tell. Fortifying herself, she continued.

"Marci was soon totally asleep and unaware of anything going on around her. The guys sprinkled some liquor on her so that she would smell like alcohol and anyone who came near her afterward would think that she was drunk. I don't even want to say what was supposed to come next, but I'm sure you can imagine how they were going to video her in a compromising situation. I never would have agreed to let them do any real physical harm to Marci, but they were going to make it look like she had gotten drunk and lost all her inhibitions. It was a total setup.

"When one of the guys sat down on the side of the bed and started to unbutton her blouse, I suddenly got sick to my stomach. I knew I couldn't let it happen. The whole scheme was just crazy. I simply could not believe that I was taking part in something so ugly and evil. What we were doing was not just mean and dirty, it was criminal. I thought about how Bradley had already ruined Junior's life and my mother's life. There I was, about to let him victimize Marci, me and the two guys he was paying to do this terrible thing.

"It dawned on me that Bradley was using me and the guys to do his dirty work with no concern for the fact that he was turning us into criminals. I didn't want to spend the rest of my life looking in a mirror and having a criminal stare back at me. It was as though a light came on in my mind. I saw clearly what was happening. Bradley was perfectly willing to throw all four of us under the bus for Junior's sake. I finally understood that Bradley would never love me like a real daughter. He only has enough room in his heart for Junior. I realized I'd been trying all my life to earn Bradley's love and approval. It was time to stop because it was useless.

"It was bad enough that Marci had been drugged already, but I was determined to save her from the rest of the plot. I only wished I had realized how stupid the whole idea was from the beginning. Now I wish I had gone straight to you, Judge Atwater, and told you what Bradley was scheming. But I was too much of a coward then."

"I wish you had come to me, too, Casey. But tell me what happened next, after you came to your senses," the judge replied.

"I immediately called it off. I took the disposable phone Bradley had given the guys to use, paid them the money he had given me to pass on to them and told them to get out and keep their mouths shut about the whole thing.

"Thankfully, they agreed and left without any argument. They'd gotten their money, and that was all that mattered to them. I didn't want to leave Marci there alone in that condition, so I stayed, praying no one would come to that room and find us. I let her sleep while I sat in a chair by the bed and tried to figure out what I was going to say when I got home and had to face Bradley. I figured he'd be furious that we hadn't carried out his orders, but I had come to the place that I just didn't care anymore.

"At some point, I dozed off in the chair. When I woke up at about 2:15 in the morning, Marci was still asleep, but I could hear that there were still a few partiers laughing and talking downstairs. I knew I had to get Marci out of there before they all left, so I called a taxi and began trying to get Marci to wake up. I wiped her face with a cold cloth and managed to get her off the bed and into a chair.

"I watched out the window for the taxi, and when I saw it coming up the driveway I grabbed hold of Marci, and we started slowly making our way down the stairs. She was still so groggy I had to support her all the way. Fortunately, no one was in the foyer as we stumbled out the front door and into the cab, so I'm pretty sure nobody saw us.

"I didn't want to send her home alone in that condition, so I had the driver to drive past my house and take Marci home first. Then I asked him to help her to your door while I waited in the car. I felt bad that the taxi driver saw Marci in that condition, so I told him she was the victim of a practical joke . . . that she didn't drink, but someone spiked her ginger-ale and it made her sick.

"Then I prayed all the way back to my house that God would help me be able to stand up to my stepdad and tell him what I had done. I wanted to tell him how despicable it was to have ever dreamed up such a rotten scheme and how I would never again let him involve me in his dirty work.

"That was my plan. But, as I was coming into the house, he was rushing out. He said something had come up at the plant, an emergency of some sort, and he told me to lock the phone in the safe, which I did after he was gone. All he asked me was, 'How did it go?' What I said was, 'It went much better than planned, as far as I'm concerned, but we need to talk about it.' He said, 'Not now. We'll talk about it later. I've got to get to the plant.'

"Apparently he hasn't even looked at the phone since then to find that the video doesn't exist, and I never knew if he actually contacted you and tried to threaten you with it. He never mentioned it to me again. But when Junior got sentenced to only one year in prison and Bradley looked so pleased with himself, I figured he must have. I'm not questioning your ruling, Judge Atwater. I believe you're an honest man. I'm sure you had your reasons and did what you thought was right. But I've been feeling guilty ever since that day because of what Marci went through and because of what you may have thought she did.

"What I'm telling you is simply that Marci has nothing to fear," Casey stated emphatically. "There is no video, never has been, and all she did was sleep. I can assure you that Junior's friends never touched her in a bad way because I didn't let them, and they did not come back after I sent them away. To be sure they didn't, I locked the bedroom door behind them and stayed with Marci until I brought her home."

Casey paused and spoke more softly. "I've told you all this because I wanted you to know exactly what took place that night. The last thing I have to say to you is that I'm deeply sorry for the trouble I helped to cause. Marci didn't deserve any of this. She's a good girl from a fine family. I truly respect her and want to be her friend. I just hope I haven't spoiled all chances of that. If you want to punish me for what I've done, I understand. I don't expect you to excuse me, but I do hope you'll forgive me."

The men looked on silently as Casey finished her detailed account and humbly bowed her head. It was obvious to them that she sincerely regretted her part in Bradley's scheme. The judge breathed a deep sigh of relief. He was convinced that Casey was telling the truth and that Marci was in no danger of being exploited by some vulgar video. Now, the judge must decide what to do with this new information.

CHAPTER 15

*B*radley Clemons definitely had more enemies than friends. If he thought everyone would just bow down meekly to his wishes and underhanded ways of getting what he wanted, he had another thought coming. A few of those enemies, whose businesses had been driven away by the big "bully" on the block, were determined to get their revenge. When Bradley had jerked the rugs out from under their establishments, their livelihoods and their families were greatly impacted. Most of them had not been able to fully recover to their former level of earnings and financial security. These men had counted on their businesses to provide food, clothing, shelter, health care, education and all the other needs of their families. Not only had Bradley wronged the business owners, but also their employees whose jobs were taken away.

Each of the businessmen who had been driven off the sizeable square block now dominated by Clemons Garment Factory had been simmering in his own pot of stew for the last several years, since they had been uprooted or, as in most cases, totally put out of business. Now, thanks to Clarence Brown, the former owner and manager of the Corner Café and the latest victim of Bradley's plant expansion, they had joined forces to bring about the downfall of Bradley Clemons' financial empire.

Every third Thursday morning of the month they met for breakfast at the IHOP on Industrial Parkway at eight o'clock. They had been meeting now for six months, and their number had grown from three to seven. The newest member of the group was Tom

Wong, who had once operated a thriving dry cleaning business on what was now referred to cynically as "Bradley's Block." When Tom walked into the pancake house at eight o'clock sharp, he joined the group of men seated around a large table in the corner at the back of the dining area just as Clarence Brown was rehashing how Bradley Clemons had destroyed his Corner Café.

"I kept a clean kitchen. You can ask anybody who ever worked for me. The health department always gave me good ratings. But when I didn't take Clemons' last offer, which was about half what my property was worth, suddenly rumors started getting out that we had rats as big as a man's fist and roaches as big as a man's thumb crawling around on everything in the kitchen and even showing up in the eating areas. There was nothing to it, but business started dropping off. Then, one morning I came in early and found the garbage cans out back overturned. Trash and food scraps were scattered all around, and there were rats and roaches crawling all over it. A photographer from the newspaper was there and a health inspector. They had gotten an anonymous tip that they could find evidence of the filth in my place if they would come on down to the café right then. They did, and I was ruined.

"Now I ask you. Is there any doubt about who set that up? Do you think I could ever open up another restaurant in this town after that picture and story got splashed all over the front page? No, I had to take Clemons' offer, and I was lucky to get a job working at the Iron Skillet. I took such a loss I'll never be able to get my own place again, anywhere." Clarence shook his head as he dejectedly looked into the faces of his fellow victims and knew they understood his frustration.

Having finished his story, Clarence welcomed Tom to the group. They all knew each other, but it had been a while since they had seen Tom. Tom was a quiet, gentle, Chinese man who generally kept to himself. The other men were a little surprised that he had finally decided to meet with them. They didn't need to be told Tom's story. His dry cleaners had mysteriously caught fire and burned to the ground. The fire department had concluded that certain cleaning chemicals had not been stored properly and that somehow a carelessly discarded cigarette or match by a person or persons unknown had ignited the fire.

When Bradley had shown up after the fire was extinguished, his comments to Tom were, "Well, Tom, this is terrible. I really hate this happened. But aren't you glad it wasn't your home? And, by the way, my offer for your property still stands. I'm feeling generous, and I didn't want the building anyway, just the land. You let me know your answer soon, before my offer is reduced."

Each of the small-business men had a story he could tell. All the stories followed a similar pattern. First, there was a friendly offer to buy them out (below fair market value, of course) then veiled threats, then problems with either plumbing, electrical wiring, rodents, rumors, broken equipment, infringement on parking spaces, broken windows, essential employees walking off the job . . . you name it! If it could go wrong, it went wrong.

Finally, one by one, each business had buckled under the pressure and financial losses. Each was eventually sold to Bradley, the only one interested in buying in the shadow of his "temple." Anybody with "one eye and half sense" (according to Clarence) could see that Bradley was the mastermind behind it all, but nobody could prove it. The police department was of no help. The Chief of Police could see, hear, and speak no evil of Bradley Clemons. He either had the intelligence of a fruit fly, or he was on the take ... or both!

The seven men decided it was time to bestow a name upon their fledgling organization. After a little give and take, they decided on the NBC Club. They had been laughing about their newly formed name and motto and were about to get on to the more significant matters when they were approached by two men in uniform ... police uniforms! Uh-oh!

"Good morning, gentlemen!" greeted Officer Reggie Green. "How's everybody doing this beautiful day? Are you fellows solving all the world's problems this morning?"

"Well, we haven't quite worked our way through all of them yet, but we're making headway!" Clarence replied with a grin. "You and Winston pull up a chair. Give us your input on how we can solve the world's problems!"

"Thanks, why not?" Reggie replied. He and Winston pulled up two chairs and sat down with the fraternity of frustrated failed-business owners, now dubbed the NBC Club. After the waitress had taken their orders, Reggie addressed Clarence.

"Clarence, I wish I could solve just one of the world's problems. In fact, I wish I could solve just one of Greystone's problems, its biggest problem. And I don't have to tell you fellows what that problem is. I know every one of you, and I know what you've been through. I hope you understand that I did everything in my power to help you guys find evidence that could save your businesses. I know you're angry with the police department because we couldn't do more, but, honestly, some of us really tried. Our hands were tied. Now, it's not really any of my business, and you don't have to tell me a thing, but is this gathering a planned event or just a coincidence?"

"Well, Reggie, let's just call it a planned coincidence!" Clarence, the self-appointed spokesman, replied. "We're just comparing notes on our separate, sad situations and licking our wounds together. You know how misery loves company! But I'll be honest with you. We're also a sort of 'neighborhood watch' group. We're keeping our eyes and ears open, and if we see anything illegal going on that could topple a certain crook in this town, we're going to expose it. Be assured, though, we're not up to anything unlawful, and there is certainly no law against having breakfast together and discussing current business affairs, is there?"

"Absolutely not, my friend!" Reggie answered. "As a matter of fact, if more citizens would keep their eyes and ears open and were willing to expose evil, our town wouldn't be so full of corruption. The bad guys can only go as far as the good guys allow. However, we can't have any vigilante-type stuff going on. That's not what I'm condoning. As a matter of fact, Winston and I are part of a newly-formed group that's going a step farther than just policing to clean up Greystone's corruption problem. A handful of policemen, serious about the situation, meet once a week to pray for our town. We're not allowed to have our prayer meetings at the station, so we meet at various public places and just ask God for guidance and to help us do a better job of protecting our citizens from those that exploit them for their own personal gain. Maybe you guys should put prayer on your agenda, too. It can't hurt, and I believe it's going to do a lot of good. I'm expecting God to win in the end, and I can see Him working already."

The NBC Club members were stunned. Praying policemen . . . who would have thought it? At least four of the men in the NBC Club were professing Christians, and they each wondered why they hadn't already thought to make prayer a part of their strategy. Well, it would be from now on! As a matter of fact, before the two officers left that morning, Reggie led the group in prayer, and after the officers had gone, the club's name was modified. The members unanimously voted to call their group the NBC Prayer Club . . . the Nail Bradley Clemons Prayer Club!

CHAPTER 16

Judge Nathan Atwater looked with sympathy into Casey's teary eyes as she finished giving her account of what had happened to Marci at the New Year's party. His initial feelings of anger at Casey had turned to compassion. He realized that this young woman was showing amazing courage to defy her stepfather and come forward with the truth. She was a "baby" Christian and was trying to start out her new life in Christ by doing the right thing. He must support her and not condemn.

"Casey," the judge began, "the way I feel right now reminds me of another time I felt much the same. Marci was only four years old, and I had taken her to the drugstore with me. It was during the Christmas season, and the store was very crowded. While I stood reading the label on a product I was planning to buy, I let go of Marci's hand just briefly and told her to stand right there, very still, and not to move! Within just a few moments, to my horror, I discovered she had moved. In fact she was gone! I looked all about, weaving around amongst the other customers and calling her name. As the moments turned into minutes, my panic grew. A few other people, taking in the situation, began searching and calling her name also. I was scared to death when I finally realized she was no longer inside the drugstore.

"I ran out the door to search the parking lot, and there she sat on an outside bench next to an elderly lady, chatting away, telling her what she hoped Santa would bring. Simultaneously, I had two reactions . . . joyful relief and a flash of anger. I wanted to grab Marci up and spank her bottom so soundly that she would never do such a foolish thing again, but, instead, I was so happy she was safe that I scooped her up into a tight hug and kissed her again and again. Then, I gave her a good scolding . . . and myself, as well, for having failed to watch her closely enough.

"Tonight I'm so relieved and happy to hear that nothing terribly bad happened to Marci in that bedroom and that no video exists, I want to hug you and thank you for intervening. I'm not going to scold you for your limited participation in Bradley's scheme. I think you've chastised yourself sufficiently. It took courage for you to come here and tell me these things. I admire you for that, and I accept your apology. I'm sure Marci will too.

"Now, if you don't mind, I'm going to ask you to tell Marci and her mother what you told us. In the meantime, I'd like to talk to these two gentlemen alone. We have some other matters to discuss. Would you come with me to meet my wife? Then, the two of you can go upstairs and talk with Marci," the judge concluded, as he stood from his chair.

"Yes, Judge, certainly, and thank you for your understanding." Casey rose, followed by David and Josh. The judge came around from his desk, took her hand, placed it in the bend of his arm, and escorted her, as the father of a bride would do, into the kitchen where he introduced her to his wife. Betty graciously greeted her, dried her hands on a kitchen towel, and led her up the stairs to Marci's room. Most of the burden was gone from Casey's heart and mind now that she had confessed to the judge and he had responded kindly. She hoped and prayed Marci and her mom would react accordingly.

When the judge returned to his office and again seated himself behind his desk, Reverend Williams, as before, began the conversation. "Thank you for your kind response to Casey, Judge. She's very fragile right now and afraid of what's going to happen to her when Bradley discovers she's gone against him. Bradley Clemons is a dangerous man. Since Mark's death, I've heard from many sources how corrupt he is. A number of people have come to me and shared their experiences with Clemons. It's not just a personal vendetta, because of Mark's death, that motivates Josh and me to want to bring Clemons to justice. It's for the good of the community. We're hoping Casey's story might help to him put away. Is there anything we can do to help?"

Judge Atwater decided to take Josh and David Williams into his confidence and share what he had attempted to do under the advice and supervision of the FBI. He explained how it had pained him to give Junior such a light sentence, and that he had done so only in co-operation with the FBI. He assured them that he was looking for ways to extend Junior's stay in prison to a more appropriate time period, hopefully as much as seven years, halfway between the minimum and the maximum sentences originally at his discretion.

Josh spoke up, "Judge Atwater, the last time I tried to talk to Marci she practically ran away from me. I'm not sure why, except that maybe she thought I was so angry about the sentence you delivered that I would take it out on her. She may even have thought I was somehow involved in what happened to her at the New Year's party because I was there for just a short time, and she caught me looking at her from across the room while she was laughing and talking with Casey. I'll admit that seeing your daughter in such a friendly situation with the sister of my brother's killer, and knowing that you would be the judge to rule in his case only a few days later was disturbing to me, and maybe it showed on my face. When Marci saw me watching them, I could tell that it made her uncomfortable, too.

I certainly was in no mood to party, anyway, so I was probably the first person to leave. The only reason I was there at all was because a friend practically dragged me there. I left long before any of Bradley's scheme started to play out. Part of the reason I was glad Casey wanted to tell you what happened that night was to let Marci know I had nothing to do with it. I want her to know she's always safe with me."

Judge Atwater grinned. "I'm glad to hear that, Josh. By now, I'm sure Marci is learning you were not involved. Casey's story was full of good news. What she confessed here tonight could be very helpful in putting Bradley Clemons away," the judge continued. "I don't want to mention that to her yet because she is fragile right now, as you said. But if I bring charges against Clemons for extortion, I will need her testimony in court. I can offer her immunity if she's willing to testify and perhaps a plea bargain with probation for the young man who actually drugged Marci, and his accomplice. I feel confident we can get Clemons for this particular crime, but there are other things going on with him that could be considered even more egregious. I'm not at liberty to share details, but you can rest assured that things are shaping up as the FBI builds their case."

"That's great!" Josh exclaimed. "I was beginning to think there was nothing that could be done to get some justice around here, but maybe our prayers will be answered soon."

"I'm very hopeful, Josh. I wish I could share with you more specifically what's going on behind the scenes, but I'm bound by confidentiality. Just keep praying that God will work on our behalf and that, in His timing, justice will be served."

The men rose, shook hands and the judge went upstairs to get Casey. Marci and Casey descended the stairs arm in arm. Josh felt his heart beating faster as he looked into Marci's glowing face, and she gave him a warm smile. As the threesome (David, Josh and Casey) walked toward their car, Marci called out, "Josh, that number you asked for? It's 262-5555!"

****

What the judge could not share with Josh and David Williams was his knowledge that on two occasions in the past four months a night raid had been conducted at Clemons Industrial Garment Manufacturing Plant when an anonymous informant had reported illegal gambling and prostitution in progress there. When the police arrived, they found nothing but a night crew . . . cleaning, working on machinery, and packing boxes of work uniforms for shipment. It was obvious that someone in the police department had given them a heads-up, and they had quickly and cleverly disposed of all the evidence.

Plans were underway to plant a mole on the night crew. He would be wearing a tiny camera to gather evidence . . . not for the police, but for the FBI. It was taking some time for the mole to win Bradley's confidence and to be transferred from the day shift to the night crew, but progress was being made.

CHAPTER 17

Janice could not remember having seen a more beautiful day. The sky was a clear, vibrant blue, with only a few fluffy white clouds floating lazily above. The manicured shrubs and the many varieties of hearty, colorful annuals and perennials professionally planted and groomed around her lovely home created a picture fit for the cover of *Southern Living Magazine* or *Better Homes and Gardens*. The swimming pool out back sparkled in the bright morning sunlight, and the rock-framed fountain at one end of the pool created the soothing sounds of a babbling brook.

Janice's favorite feature of the impressive grounds surrounding the house was the rose garden. She had spent many hours there weeding, trimming, fertilizing, de-bugging, and just enjoying the twenty or so varieties of prize-winning roses thriving there. It always irritated Bradley to see her working in the rose garden. He wanted the gardeners to do all of that. Someone might see Janice working in the yard and think they could not afford to hire it done. With Bradley, everything was about preserving his image of prosperity. Therefore, Janice made it a practice to work on her roses when Bradley was not around. The rose garden was her place of escape, and she enjoyed seeing something flourish as a direct result of her care and attention.

Nobody knows how many beautiful days he or she may have left to enjoy, but Janice was painfully aware that her number would be much fewer than she had hoped. There was a dreadful disease working away inside her body, slowly but surely robbing her of strength and making her breathing more difficult. She would have to carry out her plan before she became too weak to do so. It would be soon . . . very soon.

But, for now, she chose to think about other things. She had arranged to spend the day with her precious daughter. Janice had asked Casey to set aside this day to be with her mother. "I just want to enjoy my girl and spend a whole day with you," Janice had said to Casey three days earlier. Bradley was scheduled to play in a golf tournament that day, so the timing was perfect.

"Will you give me this Saturday? I want us to take a short trip, and I want you to drive. There's something I want to show you that I think you're really going to like. Oh, and don't tell anyone . . . this little trip is our secret!" Casey had been full of questions, curious about what her mother had planned for them, but Janice was keeping it all a big surprise. After a light breakfast together, they would take off on Janice's "mystery trip." Casey was excited.

At eight o'clock Janice and Casey were on their way. They had taken Janice's Mercedes, and Casey was driving. That was a rare treat for Casey, who usually drove the Mazda that Bradley and Janice had given her on her eighteenth birthday. Casey was thankful that Bradley had gotten her a car, even though it was about half the price and "wow-factor" of Junior's Corvette. She didn't expect to be on equal footing with Junior. She was the stepchild and had never been lavishly pampered to the degree that Junior had. But Casey was not in the least jealous of her stepbrother, whom she loved dearly. Her own father had never loved her nor supported her at all, so the things Bradley provided, though not always cheerfully, were especially appreciated. She got to live in his beautiful home, wear nice clothes, enjoy good food, and go to college. She was fortunate, and she knew it.

But there were two things Casey had yearned for and had never received from her stepfather. The first was his name. Though she had lived under his roof for twenty years, Bradley never attempted to legally adopt her. Once, when she was about eight years old, she overheard her mother and Bradley having a heated argument on the subject of her adoption. She heard Bradley yell at Janice, "I've paid for all your kid's living expenses for six years because you don't have the backbone to sue your ex for child support. Now you want me to make it legal for her to share any inheritance that would go to Junior if something happened to me? I don't think so! If you want more for Casey, go get it from her deadbeat dad!"

"But Bradley, you know he has nothing. He's become an alcoholic and a drug addict. He can't keep a job, and I don't want him in Casey's life. She's better off not knowing him," Janice had reasoned.

"Well, that's not my problem. I'll pay her bills while she lives under my roof, but that's all I'm promising. That should be enough, and don't ever bring it up again or I'll stop doing that much! Then you can get a job yourself and take over paying her expenses. How would you like that?" Bradley had shouted his ultimatum and then stormed out of the house.

To Casey's knowledge, the subject was never discussed again. However, people who knew the family seemed to assume that Casey was adopted by Bradley, because they almost always referred to her as Casey Clemons. The family never bothered to correct them; it was a little embarrassing to acknowledge and easier to let it slide. On legal documents, school records, etc., Casey was Casey Ellis. In everyday conversations, she was Casey Clemons.

The second and more important thing that Casey did not receive from Bradley was his love. The fatherly affection that she had longed for was never there. He was not especially mean to her, just indifferent, dismissive and unavailable. What made her sadder than that, though, was the obvious fact that Bradley no longer felt any affection for her mother. Janice and Casey seemed to have an unspoken pact that they would love each other enough to make up for the lack of it from the men in their lives. And today was going to be their day, a special mother/daughter day . . . a day to remember!

CHAPTER 18

The campus of Easterling College was alive once again with youthful, energetic students. As always, summer enrollment had amounted to a small fraction of the usual fall enrollment numbers. Predictably, late August had produced a new crop of freshmen, excited to begin; a returning company of seniors, eager to finish; along with sophomores and juniors in between. Josh was finally a senior; Marci was a junior.

Autumn had arrived, and the huge oaks scattered about the campus were sporting their fall colors. But the most breathtaking scene was the long, winding brick lane that led from the main road into the campus, right up to the administration building. On both sides of that road were full, perfectly-shaped Bradford Pear trees showing off such splendid color that Greystone residents made special trips to the campus just to see the trees and to take photos of their students, their small children, their bridal parties, and even their pets flanked by the stunning display of brilliant leaves.

Josh and Marci had talked several times on the phone and had met for lunch on one occasion before the fall semester began. Every day since classes had started, they each kept an eye out for the other any time they were walking across campus, in the library, in the cafeteria, or any other place where the other might happen to be. They clearly liked each other a lot, but were trying not to push the relationship too fast. Still, it was much easier every morning for each of them to get out of bed early and get to school on time, knowing the other would be close by during the day.

Studying, on the other hand, was becoming more difficult as their thoughts often wandered in anticipation of seeing each other. Josh decided that the best remedy for that would be to meet Marci at the campus library as often as they could to study together. At least that way he would not be constantly watching the door and hoping Marci would "just happen" to come in. Marci agreed to study with Josh after classes from four o'clock until whenever (usually about five-thirty or six) every Monday, Tuesday, and Thursday. The study sessions were not exactly dates, but they were the most guarded and anticipated "appointments" on their schedules.

Josh was busy on Saturdays teaching the guitar students he had inherited from Mr. Murray. The students were responding well to Josh, and he was enjoying the experience. He often thought about how God had blessed him with this job and how foolishly he had behaved last summer while working with the lawn service. In his anger and thirst for revenge, he had watched the Clemons house and studied the family's moves, which had only fueled his bitterness. One implacable, vengeful plan after another had played out in his mind until, one by one, he had rejected them all when it came time to actually commit the deeds. Finally, it seemed there was only one way to deal with his all-consuming hatred for Bradley Clemons Senior and Junior . . . God's way.

Josh had also watched the Atwater home, hoping to see Marci and confront her about her dad's connections with Bradley Clemons. He had spent time at the walking track in the park, expecting to see Marci on the adjacent tennis courts where she usually worked giving tennis lessons during the summer. He didn't want to hurt her, but he did want to talk to her about her dad and ask why he went so easy on Junior Clemons. That was probably foolish, but at that time Josh was so filled with grief and anger he felt he had to air his frustrations to the only person he knew that was close to the judge and may be willing to listen to him. Josh was puzzled when he never saw her at her home, at the park, or any place else he had looked for her throughout that first summer following Mark's death.

Now Josh knew that Marci had gone away for the summer. She remained confused and humiliated concerning what had happened at the New Year's party, fearful that any day she and others may be getting the dreaded video message by phone or by email. The pressure of "waiting for the bomb to go off" was ever present. So, as soon as the school year ended, her parents had arranged a diversion that would help distract her from those fears. They had sent her to be a camp counselor at a facility for special-needs children, most of whom had Down syndrome. Serving those sweet children for the summer had filled her with such a sense of purpose and joy that her own problems faded into the background. She had returned to Greystone with the courage to face whatever might become of the party incident, but Rev. Williams, Josh, and Casey had removed that burden altogether the night of their visit to the Atwater home.

Josh had moved beyond bitterness. Marci was free from fear. Casey had met the Savior. It had been a miraculous summer . . . a time of deliverance. God was at work, changing and mending hearts in

Greystone. But some hearts remained unchanged, as hard and cold as ever.

CHAPTER 19

Junior got a letter from Casey. He was always glad to hear from her. He wished he could see her, but he knew that his dad had forbidden her to travel to the prison and visit with him. In fact, Junior was quite disappointed that none of his family came to see him. Bradley had made it clear that he would not be seen entering or leaving such a place, nor would he allow Janice and Casey to go there. He didn't want any bad publicity, perhaps a picture and a sob story about his visiting his son in prison, showing up on the front page of the *Greystone Gazette*. So, he restricted his contact with Junior to letters and phone calls, mostly the latter. He assured Junior that if he kept his nose clean, he would be out in one year, and the time would fly by.

The nine months of incarceration that had passed were definitely without wings. They had crept by sluggishly at a snail's pace. Just to pass the time of day and the long, quiet nights, Junior found himself having to actually **think** about his life, his future, and his choices. His cellmate, Richard, had gotten a New Testament for Junior, and after much procrastination, Junior had actually picked it up one night and begun to read. He had many questions about what he read and was constantly asking Richard to explain certain passages. But, the more he read, the more he wanted to read. He certainly did not tell his dad about his new-found reading interest. Bradley would have scoffed and called him a "sissy," among other things. But, with the alcohol out of his system and with Bradley's influence over him more remote, Junior's "vision" was beginning to clear up. Casey's letter brought even more clarity to Junior's perspective.

"Dear Junior," Casey's letter began. "I hope this letter finds you feeling well. My heart breaks to think of you behind bars and lonely. I want you to know that I pray for you every night before I go to sleep and several times throughout each day. You are never far from my thoughts.

"Does it shock you that I would talk about prayer? Well, it's still a little shocking to me, too, but I must tell you that I have had a life-changing experience. Please don't tune me out, but listen to what I have to say with an open mind. It's important.

"I have become good friends with Josh Williams. I know that's hard to believe, too. Josh listened and gave me good advice when I desperately needed it. Along the way, we began talking a lot about spiritual things, a subject I had given little thought. Eventually, he took me to see his dad who, as you know, is a pastor. Pastor Williams showed me some things in the Bible that explained to me the emptiness I had always felt inside. He showed me that I was a sinner, like everyone else, and that when Jesus died on the cross He did it to provide forgiveness for my sins. He showed me verses in the Bible that said if I would believe on Christ and give myself to Him, I would be forgiven and would go to heaven when I die. Not only that, Pastor Williams told me that God wanted to be my Heavenly Father and to guide me all the rest of my life, helping me to make right choices so that my life would be worthwhile and meaningful.

"Junior, what struck me the most was to learn that God wanted to be my Father. I've always wanted a real father. Bradley has provided me with material things, but he has never loved me. My own biological father deserted me and has never cared what became of me. All my life I've wanted a father to love me and care about me. Now I have one! When I accepted Christ as my Savior, God became my Heavenly Father. I cannot tell you how happy that makes me! I know that I will still experience problems in my life, but I won't have to face them alone. God will be with me to help me. Knowing that gives me a feeling of peace like I've never experienced before.

"That's what I want for you, Junior. That's what I'm praying for. Pastor Williams has sent you several letters on this subject. He's a very forgiving, compassionate person, and despite what happened to his son Mark, he wants to help you. I don't know if you've read his letters, but if you haven't, please do. He's hoping you will write back to him with any questions you may have. He's even willing to come to the prison if you will allow him to see you.

"I love you, little brother, and I will keep praying for you. Please write back whenever you can. Casey."

When Junior finished reading Casey's letter, his eyes were moist and a lump had formed in his throat as he struggled to fight back the tears. There was a strange sensation in his heart, one that a believer would have recognized as "conviction." Junior knew that the moment of decision was very near. He must decide whether he was going to accept all this stuff about Jesus or forever reject it. He was close, very close, to deciding, but somehow he couldn't take the leap just yet.

Turning to Richard, Junior extended Casey's letter to him, indicating that he wanted Richard to read it. When Richard took the letter, Junior announced matter-of-factly, attempting to shrug off his emotions, "It's not fair. You guys are ganging up on me!"

CHAPTER 20

"Hey, Clarence, this is Fred . . . just checking in."

"Good. What's up?"

"I'm trailing her. She's headed north on the Interstate."

"Okay, Fred. You need to stay close enough that you don't lose her, but not so near that she'll notice you."

"I know that, Clarence! I'll call you back when she gets where she's going. Wait a minute, she's pulling off. Just hang on . . . . Oh, yeah, the eagle has landed!"

"Don't you mean the 'peacock'?"

"Yeah, that's good! She does know how to strut!"

"Where did she land?"

"Motel 6 on the edge of town. She's going in the office now. Looks like he's making her book the room. As always, he's watching out for himself . . . no paper trail leading back to him! All the rooms have outside access. I'll watch to see which one she goes to. Man, you'd think he could afford a fancier love nest! I guess his lovebird is not very high-maintenance!"

"Whatever! Find a place to park where you won't be obvious, and get your camera ready. I expect she'll be having company soon. Gotta go now. Call me when he gets there." Clarence hung up his phone and went on about his business while he waited to hear from Fred.

Twenty minutes later Clarence's cell phone rang. "Well, the buzzard has landed! The peacock and the buzzard are together in Room 19."

"Did you get pictures?"

"Oh, yeah! Got her going in, him going in, and the both of them as she opened the door for him . . . . Oh, crud!"

"What do you mean, 'oh, crud'? What happened?"

"Now, Clarence, don't get mad . . . . I forgot to take the cap off the lens."

"Fred, you blockhead! Some detective you are! I can see it now . . . a peacock, a buzzard and Daffy Duck! Honestly, you could mess up a one-car funeral procession! I knew I should've gone myself!"

"Well, just keep your shirt on. All is not lost. I'll just stay around until they leave and get the pictures then. Plan *b,* no problem!" Fred reasoned.

"Well, for Pete's sake take the lens cap off **now** and leave it off! Try to get it right this time, Fred. Call me when you're done."

Fred hunkered down behind the wheel of his aging Ford Taurus and watched the door of Room 19 intently. The minutes slowly ticked by with no sign of activity. Fred, who had not slept well the night before, began to fight sleep in his sun-warmed vehicle. Finally, he dozed off into a deep slumber. His head was cocked back, his mouth wide open, and his snoring could be heard several feet from his car. Fred continued to catch up on his beauty sleep until a vigorous rap on his window jarred him into consciousness. He bolted up in his seat to find the face of a middle-aged man positioned just inches from his own face. They were virtually nose to nose with only the glass between. Fred lowered his window slightly and waited to hear what the man had to say.

"Hey, fella'," the man began, "what are you doing out here?"

"Oh, nothing . . . . I'm uh, just, uh, waiting for somebody," Fred stammered.

"Well, here's the thing. If you're going to sleep here, you need to get a room," the man replied.

"Oh yeah?" Fred got defensive. "And just who are you?"

"Tom Bodett!" the man replied with a crooked grin.

"Oh, that's cute!" Fred responded sarcastically.

"Glad you think so, but enough with the chit-chat." The grin faded, and the humor in his voice vanished. "Let me be clear. You get a room or get going . . . NOW!"

"Okay, okay! I'm going! For Pete's sake, I wasn't bothering anybody. There's no need to get huffy." Fred clearly buckled under the authoritative tone and demeanor of the stranger, cranked his car and involuntarily deserted his post.

When the faded Taurus was totally out of sight, the daunting stranger (alias Tom Bodett) walked briskly across the motel parking lot and onto an adjacent parking area. There he entered the van where his partner was waiting, a van on which was painted a plumbing company's large and colorful logo.

"Well, there goes Super Sleuth!" commented *Tom*. "Do you think he could have a future with the Bureau?"

"Sure," replied the partner with a grin. "You're retiring soon. I'll take him on as my new partner. It'll be a step up for me!"

"Thanks, wise guy! I love you, too!" *Tom laughed.*

****

Across the side street a redhead wearing a blonde wig and dark sunshades sat in a borrowed car. She had followed Bradley at a safe distance and parked behind an empty church, hidden from view. No one was there on a Saturday morning. She parked at just the right angle to see clearly with her small but powerful field glasses as Bradley Clemons met his latest girlfriend at the Motel 6.

Just as I suspected . . . he's found somebody else. He never intended to marry me. How dare he use that same old excuse with me that he pulled so often on his wife when he was meeting me at various places . . . golf tournament, indeed! Can't say I'm really surprised, but what I want to know is who else is so interested in Room 19 and why? That guy in the Taurus may be working for Bradley's wife. He needs lessons! I spotted him from the get-go! But who's that in the van? That looks like trouble to me . . . professionals for sure, but certainly not professional plumbers! It could be the State or the Federal Bureau of Investigation. But why would they be watching Bradley . . . unless they're on to his business shenanigans and building a case? It wouldn't be the local police, for sure. He's got them in his back pocket.

I think the party's almost over. I'd better get out while the getting is good, thought Taressa. *If Bradley goes to prison for fraud, income tax evasion and no telling what else, he'll take me with him. Maybe I can turn state's evidence and save myself. I just hope it's not too late!*

Taressa headed straight to her office at Clemons Enterprises to start copying documents. Come Monday morning, she was calling the FBI.

CHAPTER 21

Casey and Janice were enjoying the beautiful drive to their secret destination. Janice directed Casey as she drove her mom's Mercedes out of Greystone and west on Highway 31. Early fall had always been Janice's favorite time of year. She drank in every colorful scene and stored it in her mental photo album. She recorded the sound of her daughter's voice and laughter in her heart. She hoped with all her might that Casey would be able to remember all the lovely details of this day in the years to come, for Janice would not be here to remind her. On that thought she must not dwell, or the day would be ruined. No, for once she would not regret the past nor fear the future. For one glorious day, she would just **live**.

Having driven for about thirty-five minutes, mother and daughter came into the small town of Midvale. "I've always liked this little town," Janice commented. "What do you think about it, Casey?"

"Oh, I like it, too. I went to Easterling with several Midvale students. They were nice kids. I even came here for a birthday party once and had a great time. The people seem very friendly," Casey replied. That was the response Janice had hoped for.

"When you get to the third traffic light, turn left." Janice instructed. Casey did as told, observing the quaint little shops and neat sidewalks that lined Main Street along the way. At the third light, she turned left onto Dogwood Lane. It was a Norman Rockwell sort of scene. The homes were typical middle-America, tended with great care. Lawns were well kept; colorful mums and pansies bloomed in almost every yard. Children rode their bikes in the cul-de-sac and played happily in their yards. There were even a few white picket fences here and there, many with flowering vines or climbing rose bushes adorning them with colorful blossoms and deep green foliage.

"Wow, what a lovely neighborhood!" Casey exclaimed. "It's not extravagant, but to me it just seems that real people with real lives live here. Are we visiting someone who lives on this street?"

Janice did not answer the question, but simply directed Casey to pull into a particular driveway leading to a charming, white, frame house with green shutters and an inviting porch that spanned the entire width of the house. At one end of the porch sat a pair of wooden rocking chairs painted to match the shutters. Between the rockers was a round, white, wrought-iron table on which was placed a large pot of bright red geraniums. At the other end of the porch was a green wooden swing, facing the street, flanked by two matching plant stands, each of which also supported a pot of eye-catching red geraniums. On the green door hung a large grapevine wreath tastefully decorated with large silk sunflowers and a bright, full bow made with many loops of wide ribbon fabric printed in colors of yellow, orange and red, finished off with three short ribbon streamers. The ambiance emanating from the entire structure was that of a warm, friendly welcome.

As Casey steered the Mercedes up to the carport beside the house and turned off the ignition, Janice said, "Let's go inside. I have a story to tell you, and this is the place I should tell it. You'll understand why very soon."

Janice and Casey stepped up onto the porch, and Janice retrieved the front-door key from her purse. Casey was bubbling over with curiosity and the impulse to continue probing for a quick explanation. She decided to curb her questioning and simply allow her mother to reveal her secrets at her own pace. It took the kind of self-control required to endure patiently when a long-winded friend, devoted to details, relates an extended but captivating monologue that begs the plea, "Please, get to the point!" or "Please, just tell me what happened!" *Dragnet's* Sgt. Joe Friday would say, "Just the facts, ma'am!"

The inside of the home was every bit as inviting and cozy as the exterior. After a brief tour of the unoccupied, but fully and tastefully furnished three-bedroom, two and one-half bath home, Janice invited Casey to sit with her in the window-walled sunroom on the back of the house. She brought Casey and herself a canned cola from the refrigerator, seated herself beside Casey on the cushioned glider, took a deep breath and began her story.

CHAPTER 22

"Casey," Janice began, "you were probably too young to remember any of this, but when you were about four years old and Junior was about two, Bradley and I got married. I had been taking care of Junior since he was only a few months old because his mother, my friend Kate, died shortly after his birth. That much you already knew. But there was another person who was occasionally a part of our lives too. She was Bradley's aunt, Myra Sue Craig. She was Bradley's mother's sister.

"Myra Sue married a career Marine named Joseph. Joseph was killed in a freak accident during training maneuvers just three years after their marriage. Joseph was the love of her life, and she never remarried and never had children. Myra Sue went back to college and got her degree in elementary education and began teaching right here in Midvale. She taught school for over thirty years and was well known in this area, and greatly respected.

"Aunt Myra used to visit us occasionally when Bradley and I were first married and living in a small house across town from where we live now. Bradley was struggling to build the business, and I was taking care of you and Junior at home. Money was tight, but Aunt Myra was generous and often sent or brought us a little money to help tide us over the rough spots. She continued that until one day when you were about seven and Junior was about five.

"Bradley had always been lenient with Junior, letting him have his way when he cried or pouted and refusing to spank him or discipline him in any meaningful way. He tended to think the naughty little things that Junior did were cute and just laughed them off. Sometimes he would scold Junior in a feeble sort of way but be visibly amused by his misbehavior at the same time. That sent mixed messages to Junior who would continue with his acting out.

"Well, Aunt Myra was a schoolteacher, from the 'old school,' and that kind of discipline didn't set well with her. She could see it causing Junior to become disrespectful and disobedient. She attempted to talk to Bradley about the matter, and Bradley became furious. Aunt Myra, trying to keep the peace, backed off and did not pursue the subject any further.

"Not long after that heated discussion Aunt Myra came to visit us again. The four of us were out in the backyard, Aunt Myra and I watching you and Junior play. After a while, the little boy next door came over to play too. He had just received a new Transformer toy, one that Junior did not have in his collection yet. The neighbor boy was very generous and allowed Junior to play with it for a long time. Both boys had a passion for those small toys that could be twisted and turned to take on a different form. They were all the rage with little guys at that time.

"When the neighbor boy's mother called over the fence for him to come home, he asked Junior for his toy. Junior wouldn't give it to him. I had gone inside to check on the supper that was cooking in the oven, so Aunt Myra tried to convince Junior that is was wrong to keep someone else's things without permission and that he must give it back, but he would have nothing of it. He started throwing a tantrum. I could hear him from the kitchen. Finally, Aunt Myra just took the toy from Junior's hand and gave it to the other little boy who then turned to leave. Junior chased after him, shoved him to the ground and snatched the toy away from him.

"Well, that was just more than Aunt Myra could tolerate. She reached out and gave Junior two or three harmless swats on his bottom, told him to give the toy back and to tell the little boy he was sorry for hurting him. All this happened just as Bradley came walking through the gate and as I came out the back door. Bradley was fit to be tied, not because of what Junior had done, but because Aunt Myra had dared to 'spank' Junior! He ordered her off his property and told her that if she ever came to our house again, he would have her arrested and charged with child abuse. Then he told Junior to get in the car . . . they were going to buy him a Transformer toy just like the kid's next door. Aunt Myra left, never to return. Her last words to Bradley were, 'If you ever have to go visit Junior in prison, you'll have yourself to thank for that. God have mercy on both of you!'

"A few weeks later, Aunt Myra wrote Bradley a letter and confessed that she had over-stepped her bounds by spanking Junior, but explained how her sense of justice for the little boy next door had taken uppermost place in her mind, and that the proper person to have administered a spanking would have been Bradley or me. She stressed that a five-year-old was old enough to know better how to treat his friends. In her opinion, Junior had reacted more like a toddler who had not yet learned how to share and to respect another's ownership, and she found that very disturbing. She saw that as anti-social behavior that needed to be addressed before it worsened. She begged Bradley to get counseling for the both of them. A family counselor, she suggested, might be able to help Bradley understand why he was not able to bring himself to discipline Junior. She asked if she might again be allowed to visit with the family because she did deeply love both you and Junior. Bradley threw the letter away and did not respond. He told me that she would never be allowed in our home and that I could not take you or Junior to visit her. That was his way of punishing her.

"However, he never said I could not go to see her alone, and I did . . . about once a month all these years. But, of course, I didn't tell Bradley. I brought her pictures of you and Junior from time to time and told her all about what and how you were doing. She kept all those photos, school programs, and other mementos in a special album. She even attended your high school graduations, but sat in the back where Bradley would not see her. Although she had many students along the way who were very close to her, she never stopped caring about you and Junior.

"Myra Sue had a special place in her heart for you because she knew that Bradley would not adopt you and never gave you the attention and affection that he heaped on Junior. She wanted to be sure that when you finished college and started out on your own you would have a little nest egg to help you get established. She set up a trust fund for you. You have a nice little bank account now that you can start drawing from whenever you're ready.

"Aunt Myra spent the last year of her life in a nursing home, and three months ago she died. Bradley and I were notified, but he would not come with me to her funeral. At the cemetery I met her attorney, who was also a personal friend of hers. He called me a few days later and told me that Aunt Myra had left her house, this house, and all its contents to me. I've been here several times since then, getting the house cleaned out and in order. I wanted it to look its best for you today. I have also had some papers drawn up for us to sign. I'm giving the house to you."

Casey could not speak. Her mouth fell open, and her eyes widened in amazement and disbelief. After a few moments of stunned silence, she suddenly burst into tears.

"Oh, Mother, that's one of the saddest stories I've ever heard! I'm so sorry I couldn't be here for Aunt Myra and return her love. I feel so sad that I can't thank her for her generosity. What can I do? I want to be happy, but this breaks my heart! And why do you want to give me the house? Why don't you keep it? It's not right for you to give it to me!" Casey spoke brokenly through her tears.

"I understand how you feel, sweetheart, but Aunt Myra would only want you to be happy. She lived a very full and rewarding life. If you had been at her funeral you would understand that. One person after another spoke of what a blessing she had been to them and how much they loved her. She was not without affection and appreciation throughout her life. When I would visit her in the nursing home, her guest book always had many new names since my last visit. She had a very outgoing, friendly disposition, and people gravitated to her. Unlike many people, she was neither lonely nor neglected, even in her old age and failing health. It's true that never having children of her own was a great disappointment to Aunt Myra, but many parents do not fare as well as she did in their sunset years, despite having children to care for them. So, don't be sad for Aunt Myra. It pleased her greatly to do these things for us.

"And as for the house, I have my own reasons for wanting it to be yours. The main reason is that, for now, I don't want Bradley to even know about it, much less be able to claim interest in it. If it's in your name, he cannot make me sell it and share the money with him. And, if something were to happen to me while the house is mine, it would go to him. I would want it to go to you. So, we just need to go ahead and take care of that now so there will be no question about whose it is when I'm gone. Besides, I just want you to have a place of your own. You need to get out from under Bradley's roof and be your own person. It's time you became independent. You've finished school, and you should be able to find a teaching job somewhere in this vicinity. If you don't want to stay in Midvale, you can sell the house and buy one somewhere else. That's entirely up to you. I think you should give it some thought and not make a hasty decision.

"Now, we have a ten-thirty appointment at the attorney's office, so let's go sign those papers!" Janice happily exclaimed.

CHAPTER 23

Bradley knew that Janice and Casey had planned to be away from home this Saturday. Where they were going he didn't know and didn't really care . . . probably out shopping. However, in case they were back when he got home early from the "golf tournament," he had his excuse well-rehearsed. He would claim that it had been a four-man scramble and that after nine holes one of his partners became ill and another got a call about a family emergency and had to leave . . . so their foursome had to drop out of the tournament. "But, no big deal," he would say, "we were not playing well today anyway!" Janice would swallow that story and never know the difference. Not that he was really worried about her finding out where he had actually been all morning. Their marriage was in name only at this point, and Janice seemed resigned to that reality. As far as Bradley was concerned, it was the perfect marriage . . . he did what he wanted to do, and Janice did the same. As long as she kept her nose out of his business, they would get along just fine.

Thus prepared with a suitable alibi, Bradley stopped by his house to pick up the mail before going to his office to get the briefcase he had accidentally left behind on Friday evening. The particular piece of mail he was hoping had arrived had not. However, he immediately recognized the now-familiar font and layout of his name and address on one of the envelopes he spotted as he thumbed through the stack of mail. He could feel his blood pressure rise as he tossed the envelope aside. He was determined not to open it. Why should he bother? He already knew what was in it, that stupid drawing and poem! Somebody was apparently getting his or her jollies from sending those ridiculous jail cell sketches week after week.

His initial reaction was always the same, *I'll just ignore it. I simply will not open it!* Then, despite his best efforts, he would. He always wondered if there could be something new included . . . a different message, a threat, an offer, a blackmail proposition . . . some bit of evidence to indicate who the sender was. He didn't want to miss a clue, for sure. So, eventually, he would give in to his curiosity. Today was no different, and the note was no different. Underneath the sketch of a jail cell was the now redundant poem, *Retribution*, by Henry Wadsworth Longfellow.

The viewing of the note was followed by Bradley's customary one-word response, "&%$@!" Then, into its own box flew the note, envelope and all. He'd lost count, but he knew there were approximately forty in his collection of notes containing the disturbing drawing and the pensive poem. Someone was very determined to be a "pain in his posterior!"

****

Bradley decided to park in the back at Clemons Enterprises and run in quickly to pick up his briefcase. He was surprised to find an unfamiliar vehicle parked out back. Therefore, he cautiously and quietly unlocked and opened the rear door to the office building and entered dubiously. He could hear someone moving about in the outer office where

Taressa's desk was located. Relieved, but a little puzzled, Bradley's voice suddenly broke the silence.

"Hey, what are you doing here on a Saturday?" he asked.

Taressa nearly jumped out of her skin at the abrupt interruption to her mission. "Oh, for Pete's sake, you scared me half to death! Don't sneak up on a person like that. You could cause a heart attack!" Taressa tried to cover up her alarm as quickly as possible and hurriedly, but nonchalantly, slipped a stack of papers into the folder she had laid out on her desk. Then, as inconspicuously as possible, she slid her hand over to the copy machine and turned off the power.

"You didn't answer my question," Bradley persisted.

"Oh, I had some paperwork I wasn't able to finish up yesterday, so I thought I'd work on it a little at home tonight. I hate that feeling of already being behind on my work when I come in on Monday mornings. But what are you doing here? I thought you were playing in a golf tournament today." Taressa attempted to steer the conversation away from herself and her activities.

The alibi Bradley had prepared for Janice seemed just as suitable for Taressa, so he gave her the "song and dance" about his foursome having to drop out.

"Oh, well, that's a shame," Taressa pretended to believe his story. "But what brings you here? Did you leave some unfinished business too?"

"Actually, I left my briefcase in my office and needed some of the papers in it to look at over the weekend. Would you mind getting it for me? I need to step down the hall to the restroom." Bradley wasn't buying Taressa's story any more than Taressa was buying his. She couldn't afford to pique his suspicions by taking the folder with her. She could only hope that he was, indeed, going to "step down the hall" while she went to get his briefcase.

Willing herself not to glance at the incriminating folder, she responded, "Of course, I'll be glad to get it for you. I'll be right back!" She spoke in her most carefree manner and stepped quickly toward Bradley's office.

As soon as she was out of sight, Bradley grabbed the folder off her desk. The sly fox had not failed to notice how quickly she had shoved a stack of papers into it as soon as she had heard his voice. She was up to something, and he was going to find out just what it was. He stepped out into the hallway and opened the folder. There he found page after page of confidential numbers, ledgers that had been manipulated and falsified, documents that could send him to prison for a very long time. Whatever it was that she was up to, one thing was for sure . . . it meant trouble for him. She had to be dealt with.

Taressa bounced back into her office carrying Bradley's briefcase and immediately observed that the folder was gone. What could she say or do to explain away the contents of the folder? Her mind went blank. There was nothing she could conceive that would fool Bradley at this point. Her only recourse was to escape his wrath by some hook or crook. But she had to keep her cool and look for the right moment to flee. She knew he was capable of most anything. She was in a deep, dangerous dilemma!

Bradley stepped back into Taressa's office with the damning folder in his hands. Pretending not to notice, Taressa struggled to contain the panic that had ignited in her heart and stepped forward, cheerfully handing the briefcase to Bradley. He took it and robotically placed it on a nearby chair, never taking his eyes off Taressa, studying her expression. His eyes were ablaze with accusation, but his words oozed out, slippery with that same, syrupy sarcasm he was noted for when he wanted to toy with his victim.

"My, you've been a busy girl today," he smirked. "Shall I venture a guess as to what you're planning? I believe I can see blackmail in my future, if you have your way. Am I right? I have an idea that you're the little artist behind the notes I've been receiving over the last nine or ten months. That's about how long I've been seeing Amanda. I think I get the picture. When you found out about Amanda, you started setting me up for your little blackmail scheme. Well, I don't appreciate your artwork or your taste in poetry. You've got to be crazy if you think you can fleece me. Nobody double-crosses me and gets away with it!"

Bradley was slowly advancing closer and closer to Taressa like a jungle cat sneaking up on his prey, and his eyes were taking on a frightful glare as he approached her. Taressa inched backward toward her desk as Bradley closed in on her.

"Now, Bradley, calm down," she began trying to reason with him. "I don't know what you're talking about. Who is Amanda? I swear I don't know anything about any notes or any blackmail scheme. You've got it all wrong. Please, listen to me. I can explain everything. We can work this out. Nobody needs to get hurt here. We're in this together. You know that if you go down, I go with you. Stop and think, Bradley! You're not making any sense!" Taressa couldn't seem to stop her nervous prattle.

Terror gripped her as she detected murder in Bradley's eyes. He was zoned out with rage, and there was no getting through to him. Suddenly, she bumped against the desk in her backward retreat from Bradley who now had dropped the folder, raised his hands menacingly, and was reaching for her neck. She tried to scream, but his swift, crushing grip cut off her breath. Her arms and hands desperately flailed about on the desk behind her, grasping for anything she could find with which to defend herself. Her right hand finally reached the only object there that she might use to get him off of her. She wrapped her fingers tightly around the large, heavy, polished rock that served as a paperweight, and with all the strength she could muster she swung wildly at Bradley's left temple. The blow stunned him, and he staggered backward releasing his stranglehold on her neck, enabling her to gulp in a deep, refreshing breath.

While he was still reeling from the effects of the forceful blow, she used the desk as support and kicked him with all her might in his gut, using both feet simultaneously. The "double whammy" caused him to heave and to crumple to the floor in pain. She had managed to knock the breath out of him and gain a small window of opportunity to escape. She took a split second to grab up the folder and her purse then ran like a frightened rabbit out the back door.

Bradley slowly pulled himself up from the floor and stumbled around in a daze just long enough for Taressa to jump into the borrowed car, start it, throw it into gear and speed off, burning tire tracks into the pavement as she fled.

CHAPTER 24

As Janice and Casey rose from the glider in the sunroom where Janice had told Casey the story of Aunt Myra, Casey threw her arms around her mother and thanked her profusely for giving her Aunt Myra's house and for keeping up her friendship with Myra Sue through the years. Casey still could not take in all the wonderful things that were happening to her. It seemed that her new Father was blessing her in ways she could never have imagined. In her heart she was thanking Him over and over.

Casey had something wonderful to share with her mother, too . . . something more valuable than money or houses. She had prayed that God would show her exactly when and how to present that gift to Janice. Oh, how she prayed that today would be the day and that her mother would be willing to accept the greatest gift of all.

After locking up the house, mother and daughter walked arm in arm down the front steps and followed the walkway to their car. Both were wearing broad smiles and feeling very happy. As they were about to enter the Mercedes, a woman's voice called out to them, "Hi, there! I'd ask how you ladies are doing, but it's obvious to me your doing fine! It's nice to see folks smiling. Janice, I'm guessing this must be your daughter Casey. Am I right?" The pleasant-looking neighbor who had been sweeping off her front porch paused to greet Janice and Casey.

"Hello, Daisy," replied Janice. "Yes, this is Casey. Casey, this is Mrs. Daisy Preston. She's been a neighbor and good friend to Aunt Myra for many years. Daisy and I have chatted on several occasions. She and her son kept an eye on Aunt Myra's house while it was unoccupied, when Aunt Myra was in the nursing home. And that's just one of the ways she was a good neighbor and friend. Aunt Myra used to tell me that she and Daisy were like sisters."

"I'm glad to meet you, Mrs. Preston," Casey responded. "I'm very sorry for your loss. I know you must miss your dear friend."

"Thank you, darlin'. I certainly do . . . and just call me Daisy. That's how most folks know me, and I like it that way. Your mama told me Myra Sue's house was going to be yours and that you just might decide to live in it. I surely hope you do. I'd know I was getting another good neighbor next door, and I'm sure Myra Sue would be happy to see that . . . if she's lookin'! Of course, it may be that she's havin' so much fun 'up there' that she's got no time to be checkin' up on us," Daisy grinned warmly.

"Well, I'm glad to see you're not talking to yourself again, Mother," a smiling young man teased as he stepped around the corner of the house. "Good morning, ladies." He nodded in the direction of Janice and Casey.

"Steven, you've met Mrs. Clemons, but this is her daughter, Casey. Casey, this is my son, Steven."

Janice watched Casey's reaction as Steven approached them. It was apparent that she was impressed with his good looks. He was tall and well-built with blonde hair and green eyes that sparkled. There was an outdoorsy quality about him that made him appear healthy and wholesome . . . and that big, broad smile . . . well, it was the kind that could melt a young woman's heart! When Casey extended her hand for a handshake, Steven removed his work glove and took her hand. "I'm pleased to meet you, Steven." Casey returned his smile.

"Likewise," Steven responded. "Please excuse my appearance. I've been doing a little yard work out back. I'm not always this dirty, but I have been dirtier!" His smile grew wider. "I enjoy yard work, so if you ladies ever need some help next door, just let me know. It's nice to see you again, Mrs. Clemons, and good to meet you, Casey. I guess I'd better get back to work. Have a nice day!"

Casey watched as Steven lifted a huge bag of landscaping mulch from the edge of the porch, hoisted it over his shoulder, and headed to the back yard to continue his work. She was impressed! Who knew a strong, handsome neighbor would come with the house? Janice did!

****

Janice and Casey met the lawyer in his office and signed the necessary papers. He was very kind and accommodating to give them an hour of his Saturday morning. Now Casey was officially the proud new owner of her very first place. She wanted to go back to the house and examine every inch of it. Before she knew it was to be hers, she didn't look as closely at details as she would have, had she known. After hearing Aunt Myra's story, there had not been enough time before their appointment to tour the house and yards more thoroughly. Janice knew Casey would probably want to return to the house after the signing, so she had figured that into her plan for the day. But first, she wanted to treat Casey to lunch at a quaint little café on Main Street, Dora's Diner.

Dora Bunn, the owner and main cook, served up delicious, made-from-scratch dishes that were town favorites. Many times Janice had indulged in one of Dora's popular chicken salad croissants. She and Aunt Myra had agreed that no one could do chicken salad better. Dora took the finest cuts of boneless chicken breast and boiled them in seasoned water. When they were done and cooled, she chopped the chicken and added roasted walnuts, seedless red grapes, finely-chopped parsley, and just a little very-finely-chopped celery, along with a pinch or two of salt and pepper, of course. Then she stirred it all together with just the right amount of her own tangy, homemade mayo. Served with crackers, bread, croissants, or all by itself, it was always scrumptious. Aunt Myra used to say that Dora's chicken salad made what the grocery store sells taste like a thin, stringy celery-and-mayo spread.

But Dora's greatest claim to fame was her homemade chocolate, coconut, and lemon cream pies. The crusts were tender and flaky and baked to the perfect shade of golden brown. The fillings were smooth and luscious, and the meringues were piled high with little curled peaks, also perfectly browned. People drove from miles around to have a piece of Dora's delicious pies along with a piping hot cup of her very own special blend of gourmet coffee.

After hearing Janice's description of Dora's specialties, Casey was as hungry as a bear. She and Janice chose a table near a window so that they could enjoy the outdoor beauty as they indulged first in a chicken salad croissant with iced raspberry tea, and then chocolate pie with hazelnut caramel coffee. This was not a day for counting calories; it was a day for celebrating blessings!

The cheerful, clean, cozy atmosphere of the diner, the tasty food, and the earlier events of the day were weaving themselves together into the perfect mother/daughter day. *What better time than now,* thought Casey, *to tell Mother **my** good news?*

Over coffee and pie, Casey shared with Janice that Josh and Rev. Williams had explained to her how she could become a Christian. She described how happy she was to have a Heavenly Father and to know that God loves her. Then she asked Janice if she would like to accept Christ too. "You know, Mother, you and I have had a lot of the good things in life, but I don't think we were able to enjoy them to the fullest or use them the wisest because we've not given God His rightful place in our lives. I think we both would agree that all the things we own have not really made us happy. We can blame Bradley for dealing us misery at times, but I've learned that with Jesus in my heart I can be happy regardless of how Bradley feels about me. I want you to have that same happiness. God loves you, Mom. Jesus died for you. Wouldn't you like to belong to Him?" Casey waited patiently for Janice's response.

After a few moments of consideration, Janice replied, "Casey, I'm very glad that you're happy and that you've found something to believe in that gives you peace. I do believe that God loves some people. I certainly believe He loves you. You're a good person and easy to love. But God does not love me. I could prove that to you, but not today. This has been a cheerful day, and I want it to stay that way. So, if you don't mind, I'll just be happy for you, and we will leave it there. Okay?"

Casey's heart was suddenly broken, but she was determined not to show just how disappointed she was. She understood that it may take some time and lots of prayer for her mother to believe. Having felt unloved for so long, it would be difficult for her to accept God's love.

"Okay, Mother. I understand how you feel. But just remember this . . . the Bible says that God loves the world. That means everybody, not some people in the world or everybody in the world except Janice Clemons. Believe it or not, He even loves Bradley Clemons! So, I hope that someday you'll take God at His word and just receive His love. We'll talk some more about it another time. This **has** been a wonderful day that I will never forget, and we aren't even finished with it! The day you accept Christ will be another wonderful day! But for now, let's go back to my house and look around some more."

"Are you sure it's your new house you want to see and not your new neighbor?" Janice teased. "And I don't mean Daisy!" she added with a laugh.

CHAPTER 25

*B*radley, holding the left side of his head where a knot was quickly rising, and feeling as though he'd been kicked by a mule both there and in his stomach, staggered out the rear door of the office building into the back parking area. Taressa had sped off in the white Toyota Camry that he had seen parked there earlier. He knew he couldn't catch her, but he was hoping to see the license plate, something he now wished he'd noticed before. He could see the white car pulling into traffic too far away for him to read the tag numbers. There was no point in trying to follow her. By the time he got onto Jackson Boulevard, she could have turned off anywhere. Besides, he was in no condition to drive just yet. He knew what he had to do. Back inside the office building, he picked up the phone.

"Leonard, we've got a situation! I caught Taressa copying confidential documents. She got away from me. If she puts those papers in the wrong hands, I'm cooked. You put out an APB on her right now! We've got to get that folder full of papers back. I don't care what you have to do. Tell 'em I caught her stealing money from the safe . . . tell 'em she's armed and dangerous . . . tell 'em to do whatever it takes to stop her, and I don't care if that means a bullet in her head! She's driving a white Toyota Camry. It's not the car she usually drives, so you can't look up her license plate number, and I didn't get a chance to see it."

"Hold on, Bradley! Are you sure she's got anything incriminating? Besides, she can't hurt you without hurting herself too!" Chief of Police Leonard Hatfield didn't want to believe his ears.

"Of course I'm sure! I saw the papers . . . held them in my hands . . . and I'm telling you she's up to no good. Never mind **how** I know! I **know**! Just trust me! Stop wasting time with foolish questions and get after her!" Bradley screeched.

"Good grief, Bradley, do you know how many white Toyota Camrys there are in this town? Camrys are one of the most popular cars on the road these days . . . and you didn't even get the license plate number!"

"Listen, blockhead, if you don't shut up and get busy, you and I both will be **making** license plates for a very long time. Besides, how many of those white Toyotas are being driven by a woman with long, flashy red hair and wearing blue slacks and a white sweater? She was headed south on Jackson Boulevard. Now, you find her and get that folder for me! Don't let anybody walk away with those papers, do you understand?"

"Okay, Bradley! I'm on it! Meanwhile, you go to her apartment and see if she's there. She's going to be on the run, but she may decide to stop there first to grab some of her things. That depends on how smart and how scared she is. Don't worry. We'll find her."

****

*He tried to kill me! He **will** kill me if he finds me. I'm sure he's got the cops looking for me. I've got no place to go, no place to hide. Oh, God, help me get out of this town before I'm spotted! I don't know what to do!* Taressa was in a panic as she traveled down Jackson Boulevard knowing that at any moment a police car might pull her over. She willed herself to drive within the speed limit and to do nothing that would draw attention. *Oh God, oh God, help me!* Then it occurred to her that it seemed she was praying. She didn't think she knew how, but there it was . . . brought on by desperation.

There was a church! She had already successfully hidden out behind one church today. Maybe she should try it again. As she got closer, she could read the church sign, "God is our refuge and strength, a very present help in trouble." *Well, I'm in trouble, and I need help, so we'll just see if there's any truth to that little slogan!* Taressa reasoned skeptically.

Taressa turned onto the vacant church parking lot and drove back behind the building. She parked as close to the structure as possible and forced the frightening office scene from her mind so that she could collect her thoughts and try to come up with a plan. She remembered the tote bag she had tossed onto the back seat earlier. In it were the blonde wig and the big, dark sunshades. Also, lying on the front seat beside her was the navy blue cardigan that matched her slacks. Yes, the first thing she must do was to change her appearance so that she could evade the police as long as possible. Surely Bradley would have given them a description something like . . . *red hair, white sweater, blue slacks.*

Taressa quickly grabbed the tote bag and pulled out her articles of disguise. She twisted up her long red tresses and tucked them under the short blonde wig. Next, she donned the navy cardigan sweater over the white pullover. The final touch was the sunshades. What a stroke of "luck" that she had needed those items this morning while following

Bradley and now had them readily available to use in helping her escape from Bradley! Perhaps they would buy her enough time to get to a place of safety.

Okay, Taressa, think! So far, so good . . . but what next? I can't stay here forever. I need to get out of town, but they'll be looking for me in this car. They may even have the license number. I've got to ditch the car, but I certainly can't just go walking down the street. Okay, if I can make my way downtown, I'll leave the car in a public place and go into a store where I'm not known. Then, maybe I can catch a city bus somewhere . . . but where? Bradley knows all my friends and may be having them watched. I certainly can't go home.

While still trying to figure out what she could do after leaving the car behind, Taressa looked up and saw, with mounting distress, another car approaching. She wanted to speed away, but knew that would only arouse suspicion and may even cause this unknown person to call the police. She had to stay calm and come up with a logical explanation for her being there. The driver of the other vehicle pulled up beside her. He was facing the opposite direction, so the two drivers were only a few feet apart. The man lowered his window, as did Taressa.

"Hi, ma'am! I'm Wayne, the Associate Pastor here. May I ask why you're sitting back here all by yourself? Do you need help?"

It suddenly occurred to Taressa that all she needed to do was tell the truth, but not her whole story. "Well, to be honest, I do need help, but not the kind you can give me. You see, my boyfriend is very angry with me right now. He tried to hurt me, and I just had to get away from him. I was actually hiding back here until I could figure out what to do. It's not safe for me to go home right now. I hope you'll forgive me if I'm trespassing or something."

"No apology necessary," Wayne responded. "Listen, if you think that guy's going to hurt you, we could call the police and see what they can do to protect you. Or you could call the women's abuse hotline. They would give you shelter until you can work out your plans. I've got the number in my office if you'd like me to get it for you, or you could just call information."

"You're very kind, Wayne. I'll consider calling the hotline. I hadn't thought of that. But I don't want to involve the police. My boyfriend has too many buddies in the police department. I don't think they would choose to help me. I'll just be on my way now. Thanks for the suggestions."

"Well, I can't let you go without praying for you. Do you mind?" Wayne replied.

Taressa was taken off guard, but felt she had no choice but to comply. "Well, you need to know that I'm not really a praying person, but if you want to, I don't suppose it could hurt anything," she agreed reluctantly.

Taressa's eyes nearly popped out of her head when Wayne hopped out of his car, reached through her window for her hands, held on to both of them and poured out a heartfelt prayer for God to watch over her and keep her safe. When he closed with a strong "amen" he looked up at Taressa and smiled a big, warm grin. As he released her hands, he said, "May God go with you, and you come back to visit us on a Sunday. We'd be glad to have you worship with us. Meanwhile, if you need us to help you, please call. That's what we're all about . . . serving God by helping people." Then Wayne reached into his pocket and pulled out his wallet. "I've only got ten dollars on me right now, but I want you to take it. It might buy you something to eat or a little gasoline to help you get to safety."

Taressa tried to refuse the ten-dollar bill, but Wayne just dropped it inside her window and said, "Hey, if you don't need it, pass it on to someone who does." Then he stepped back into his car and pulled away to a designated parking space as Taressa, in a state of amazement, drove off the parking lot of Greystone Community Church and headed toward downtown.

CHAPTER 26

*I*n her study of the Bible, "forty" had always been an interesting number to Lydia Williams. When God flooded the earth, saving only Noah, his family, and the animals in the ark, it had rained forty days and forty nights.

When God took Moses up into a mountain to give him the law, called "The Ten Commandments," Moses was there for forty days and nights.

The "children of Israel," the Hebrews, because of their disbelief and disobedience wandered in the wilderness forty years before entering the "promised land."

Jesus, Himself, spent forty days and nights in the wilderness before He began his public ministry.

Lydia had spent forty weeks in her own private wilderness, wrestling with the kind of sorrow only a grieving parent can comprehend . . . the loss of a child.

Mark had died on a Thursday. He was buried on the following Saturday afternoon. Every Saturday since, Lydia had gone to Memory Garden Cemetery and visited Mark's grave. When the weather permitted, she would sit for a while on one of the concrete benches located near his grave. There she would sometimes sing a few of her favorite hymns and some of the little choruses she had sung to Mark when he was a small child. Many times she would sit quietly reading passages from her Bible about heaven and envisioning Mark there. Occasionally, she would bring her sketch pad and draw sketches of the beautiful scenery in the cemetery, for she was quite a good artist. But, always, she would pray.

Lydia prayed that God would give David, Josh, and herself the strength to bear their tremendous burden of sorrow. She prayed, though reluctantly at first, for the forgiveness and salvation of the young man who had killed her son. She prayed that righteousness would conquer evil and that somehow good would come out of Mark's death. Lydia had been a Christian and a pastor's wife long enough to have seen God, many times, take a terrible tragedy and squeeze a blessing out of it. Not that the tragedy itself ever became something to treasure and celebrate, but to witness God at work, as though refusing to let the tears of His children be wasted, had always amazed her. Now, she had been asking and expecting for forty weeks that God would redeem her tears. Somehow she felt the answer to her prayers was imminent.

Today, the fortieth Saturday, Lydia Williams stood by her son's grave and thanked God for the peace that was slowly returning to her heart, the assurance she possessed that Mark was safe and happy in heaven, that David and Josh had come a long way in their journey to recovery, and that her favorite Bible verse for many years could remain her favorite . . . *For we know that all things work together for good to them that love God, to them who are the called according to his purpose.* Romans 8:28

As she was leaving the cemetery, Lydia noticed that it was nearing noon. She knew that Josh would have an hour's break for lunch before his next guitar lesson. She decided to stop in at Madison's Music Store to see if perhaps he would like to have lunch with her. Josh was so busy with schoolwork, teaching music lessons and seeing Marci these days that Lydia seldom had time to talk to him alone. It was highly possible that he had already made plans for lunch, but she would take the chance. Besides, there were a couple of items she needed to pick up downtown; so, either way, it would not be a wasted trip.

Ten minutes later Lydia parked near the front of Madison's, walked inside and began to browse through the sacred music compact discs on display while she waited for Josh to finish teaching his eleven-thirty student and emerge from Studio 3.

****

Taressa's plan had taken a slight twist since her encounter with Associate Pastor Wayne at Greystone Community Church. As she was proceeding down Jackson Boulevard in the white Camry, she passed the city bus that went downtown. Just ahead she saw several people waiting at the next bus stop to catch that downtown bus. She had just enough time to park the Camry and join the group as the bus approached. As Taressa boarded the bus, she thought that the driver gave her a strange look.

I'm getting paranoid. I don't know the driver, and how could he possible know me? I haven't ridden public transit in years. When I get off this bus, I'll figure out who I can call to come get me, someone Bradley wouldn't think of. I don't have enough cash on me to rent a hotel room. I'd have to use my credit card . . . not a good idea. I've got to let Greg know where I left his car, too. Okay, one step at a time. For now, I'm safe!

The city transit driver was Jasper Morris. Jasper was a member of the NBC Prayer Club and he recognized Taressa. The club members knew her as the overly-dedicated, redheaded bookkeeper for Clemons Enterprises. What gave her away was the strand of red hair that had escaped the blonde wig and was, unknown to Taressa, revealing her disguise.

Jasper, who wore a hands-free cell phone headset over his left ear, had received a call from Clarence Brown about ten minutes earlier.

"Jasper, I've been listening to my police scanner. They've just issued an APB on Clemons' secretary/bookkeeper. They say she was caught robbing the office safe and may be armed and dangerous. She fled the scene driving a white Toyota Camry. It seems that Clemons is getting a little come-uppance. Interesting, huh?" Clarence had reported with a degree of satisfaction. "Anyway, I just thought I'd let you know in case you happened to see her out there . . . not that you could or should do anything about it if you did see her, but if you do, keep your head down! It could be dangerous running into a scared, redheaded female that's packin'! Talk to you later."

Having arrived downtown, Taressa decided that the bus stop up ahead was the perfect one at which she should disembark. It was smack-dab in the middle of town, and she had distanced herself from the Camry. Several other riders chose that spot to exit as well. She waited until last to step off the bus, but the driver summoned her as she was about to exit the middle door.

"Ma'am, I need to see you for just a minute, please!" Jasper called out to Taressa.

Taressa froze in her tracks. Her first impulse was to hurry off the bus and run, but something told her to stay. She stepped forward to the driver and asked,

"What's the problem, driver? Didn't I deposit the right amount of money?"

"Yes, you did," Jasper responded. Lowering his voice, he whispered, "I'm seeing red, and you should fix that," he grinned. As he spoke, he pointed to his neck behind his right ear so that she would know where to look on herself. Taressa bent down and looked at her reflection in the rear-view mirror. There, on the right side of her head, just behind her ear hung a long, tell-tale strand of bright red hair. She quickly tucked it out of sight under the blonde wig. She looked at Jasper with a questioning look, wondering why it was of any concern to him.

"Taressa, the police are looking for you. I don't believe their story for one minute. I know how Bradley Clemons lies and connives. You be careful out there!"

CHAPTER 27

When Janice and Casey returned to the Midvale house after their lunch at Dora's Diner, Janice wanted Casey to take all the time she needed to look everything over carefully. "Just enjoy getting acquainted with your new house," she insisted, "but, if you don't mind, I'd like to rest a little while, maybe just 'catnap' for a few minutes right here on the sofa. Would that be okay with you?"

"Of course, Mother. You do look a little pale," Casey replied. "I've been worried about you lately. At home, you haven't seemed as energetic and active as usual. I've noticed that you walk a little slower, and the stairs at home leave you winded. I don't think you've fully recovered from your anemia. Are you still taking your iron supplement?"

"Yes, I've been taking my iron supplement and half a dozen other supplements, too. Don't worry about me, honey. It's just that I've gotten accustomed to a little nap after lunch most days. Today has been especially exciting for me, so I'm a little more drained than usual. After thirty minutes or so of rest, I'll be as good as ever."

"Are you sure you haven't overworked yourself? I can only imagine what a big job it was to clean out a house that's been lived in for over thirty years and then left unoccupied for more than a year. Everything looks so clean and fresh, it must have taken many hours of work. It seems to me the walls have been newly painted, too. Surely you didn't do that yourself! You should have let me help with the work.

How were you able to get all this done in such a short time and without my knowing about it?"

"Oh, you're giving me way too much credit!" Janice responded. "First of all, your Aunt Myra was a good housekeeper. She wasn't one to keep a lot of useless clutter. And then, I enlisted lots of good help because, even though I'm certainly following doctor's orders, you're right . . . I've not regained all my strength. So, one or two days every week for the last three months, when you and Bradley were away for the day, I'd get Luke to drive Lucy and me here. The three of us would work together for several hours. Occasionally, Luke brought along his son, Adam, to help. Adam was especially good with the painting. I must admit, they were almost as excited about this project as I was, and they did most of the hard work. I was mainly the supervisor, shopper and planner for the job.

"Lucy was in charge of the cleaning while Luke and Adam took care of the minor repairs and the painting. You can thank that handsome young man next door for making the yard beautiful. He even put the geraniums on the porch, and he wouldn't allow me to pay him for any of it. The things in the house that I didn't want to keep, I packed up and gave to Goodwill, but I kept a few of Aunt Myra's little treasures just as reminders of her, along with her best tableware and kitchen utensils. Then I bought a few basic linens for the beds, bathrooms and kitchen. The window treatments were a little faded and dated, so I took them down and had new blinds installed.

I decided to leave the rest of the decorating to you, but basically it's move-in ready. The house is yours now, and you'll want to add your signature to the décor, especially if you decide to keep it and live in it yourself. Of course, it's your responsibility now, too. I wanted it to be in good shape when you got it, and I know you'll do a great job of keeping it up!"

"Well, Mother, you and your crew have done a superb job. Somehow, this already feels like home to me. I believe I would love living here! If I can't find a teaching job here in Midvale, perhaps I can find one in Greystone. The commute would not be bad at all.

"And, you're right, Mother. It's time for me to stop depending on Bradley and become an adult! You and Aunt Myra have given me a jump start that few people get when they set out on their own. I'm so blessed, and thankful, and excited about starting a new life! I don't even know how to express it. Thank you, Mom. I love you to the moon and back!"

Casey gave her mother a long, tender hug. "What would I ever do without you?" she mused. "You've always taken great care of me. It's time for you to rest a little and let me take care of you. We've got to get you all well and healthy again! For now, I want you to go into one of the bedrooms and take a good, long nap. We don't have to do another thing today. Besides, I'm in no hurry to leave my new home!"

****

Casey's happiness was therapy for Janice's weak, weary body and her worried mind. The first part of Janice's plan was a grand success. Her faithful housekeeper/cook, Lucy, and the dedicated handyman/butler, Luke, had made it possible. They were the only two people, other than her doctors, who knew Janice's dreadful secret. Luke and Lucy were more than household employees, they were faithful friends.

Janice had covered up her blunder at the supper table, when she almost revealed her bad news from the doctor, by telling Casey later that her doctor had discovered she was quite anemic, causing her to feel overly fatigued. That was indeed true, but that was the good news compared to the staggering news he had gone on to share with her. Her anemia due to iron deficiency could be easily treated, but the ALS would not go away. It was good to know that Luke and Lucy would be there for her when she needed help until the time was right to tell Casey. However, Janice would not be able to ask for anyone's help with the second and final part of her plan. That part would be the most difficult, and she would have to do it alone. The question in her mind was *how much longer can I wait?*

CHAPTER 28

"Hey, buddy, wake up! Hey, Junior, it's me . . . you're okay . . . wake up, pal! You must be having a bad dream. Calm down. You're okay." Richard tried to wake Junior who was yelling and screaming as though he were being attacked. It was well after midnight, and Richard was awakened from a deep sleep by Junior's sudden cries.

A guard appeared at the door of the cell. "What's going on in there? You two stop that fighting right now, or I'll put you in solitary," the guard ordered as he shined his flashlight on the two cellmates. "Levitt, get back to your bunk, **now**!"

Richard moved away quickly, as told, but Junior continued to moan and cry. "We weren't fighting. I was trying to wake him up to see why he was yelling. He's either having a nightmare, or he's sick and in pain," Richard explained.

The guard was about to call for backup so that he could go into the cell and check on Junior when Junior finally woke up out of his dream. He looked sheepishly at the other two men who were observing him intently.

"What? What are you looking at? What did I do?" Junior was in a state of confusion. He was remembering snippets of his dream, but was totally unaware that he had been reacting to it as he had.

The guard responded, "Listen, kid, you were waking up the whole joint! You must have been having one heck of a nightmare. Whatever you ate for supper tonight, you'd better skip it next time!"

"Yeah, I'll remember that. Next time I'll choose the filet mignon over the lobster!" Junior responded sarcastically, as was typical. But then he spoke with uncharacteristic sincerity, "I'm sorry I woke everybody up. I hope you can go back to sleep."

The guard and Richard, both, were surprised by Junior's civil, considerate response. They stared at him as he lay there propped up on one elbow, looking scared and vulnerable.

"Hey, who are you? And what have you done with Junior Clemons?" The guard asked. "That's the first decent thing you've said to me since you got here. Maybe you should have nightmares more often," he grinned.

Junior was thinking . . . *that just may be the first time in my whole life that I apologized to anyone. What's happening to me?*

"Well, don't get too excited . . . I think it was an accident!" Junior grinned slightly as he rubbed his eyes, took a deep breath to settle his nerves, pulled the blanket back over himself, and turned his back to the two gawkers.

The guard, satisfied that everything was okay, went back to his post. Richard lay back down and stared at the ceiling. The truth was that this was not the first night Junior had awakened him due to troubling dreams. It was just the most extreme incident yet.

"Junior," Richard whispered. "Are you awake?"

"Yeah," Junior replied.

"Want to talk about it?" Richard inquired in hushed tones.

"Tomorrow," Junior whispered back.

"Okay, I expect I'll be right here!" Richard responded and closed his eyes.

CHAPTER 29

"Thanks," Taressa replied to Jasper, the concerned bus driver. "I'll be careful, or I'll be dead! Bradley tried to kill me, and I figured he would have the police on my trail. If anything happens to me, I'm telling you, Bradley Clemons will be behind it . . . just so you know."

"Good luck!" That was all Jasper could think to say as Taressa quickly exited the bus.

Taressa looked around carefully and, at the intersection, crossed the street. She began walking down the sidewalk, trying to decide which store in which to take refuge and call her cousin who lived on the outskirts of town. She and Debra were not very close, two very different people. As a matter of fact, Taressa and Debra had not made contact with each other in over a year, which probably explained why Taressa didn't think of her right away. However, Taressa felt sure she could count on Debra for help in a crisis. Taressa had never told Bradley that she had a cousin living in Greystone; so, hopefully, he didn't know about her.

Taressa found herself in front of Madison's Music Store just as she noticed a police car in the distance, moving with the traffic in her direction. Without a moment's hesitation she reached for the door and quickly stepped inside Madison's. It was a strange place for her to be. She could neither sing nor play an instrument. However, she did like to listen to music occasionally, though not passionately. She moved to the section of the store where there were racks of CDs and began to search through the music as though she were looking for a particular one.

"Hi, may I help you find something?" the friendly young salesgirl asked.

"Oh, no, thank you. I'm just browsing," Taressa replied and continued to glance through the displays. When the young lady had moved along, out of earshot, Taressa pulled out her cell phone. Thankfully, Debra's numbers, both home and cell, were keyed into her contact list. First, she called the home number. After a few rings she heard the easily recognizable ascending three-tone pattern which preceded the message, "We're sorry. The number you have reached has been disconnected or is no longer in service. If you feel you have reached this number in error, please hang up and try your call again."

Oh, great! She's probably moved to Siberia, thought Taressa as she tried the cell number.

"Your call has been forwarded to an automatic voice message system. The person you are trying to reach is not available. At the tone, please record your message. When you have finished recording, you may hang up or press '1' for more options. *Beep.*"

"Debra, this is Taressa. Call me back, please. I need to talk to you. It's important. Thanks!" Taressa ended the call. Knowing that she may not hear back from Debra for a long while, she began trying to think of someone else to call. All the names that crossed her mind were people connected with Bradley, or they were out of town, or for some reason she did not feel comfortable asking them for help. There was no telling what people had heard about her by this time. What now?

Lydia Williams glanced down the aisle and saw the blonde-haired lady looking at CDs but thought nothing unusual about her. She was just another customer searching for some good music to listen to. Or so she thought until she saw Taressa (unaware that anyone was observing her) sigh deeply, bow her head low, and lean her body forward, bracing herself with both hands on the music rack. Her body language vividly signaled her exasperation and exhaustion. She looked like a woman at the end of her rope, and, indeed, she was. She kept trying to think of options for escape, but her mind had gone blank. Fear of being spotted at any moment by the police was interfering with her ability to reason clearly. Never before had she found herself at such a dead end with nowhere to turn.

Think, Taressa, think! She chided herself. *You can't give up now. In a town as large as Greystone, there must be somewhere you can hide safely. Oh, God, where is that place, and how can I get there?* The last question wasn't so much a prayer as it was an afterthought, but God hears everything, even thoughts and afterthoughts!

"Excuse me. I don't mean to pry, but you look like you don't feel well. Are you okay? Is there something I can do to help you?" Lydia asked gently when she arrived at Taressa's side.

Taressa was startled and straightened quickly. "Oh, no, I'm okay. Thank you. I'm just exhausted and feeling a little lightheaded, but I'll be all right. You're very kind to ask," she replied.

"Well, there's a nice seating area over there," Lydia pointed out, "where you can sit and rest awhile. Let me help you to one of the sofas. You don't need to be on your feet if you feel lightheaded. You might faint and hurt yourself in the fall." Lydia took Taressa's arm without waiting for an answer, gently led her to the parents' waiting area and seated her.

Then she went to the water dispenser and filled a paper cup with cold water.

"Here, this should help you feel better," Lydia said as she offered the cup of water to Taressa.

Taressa accepted the cup and drank the refreshing liquid gratefully. She had not realized that she was both thirsty and hungry. It was noon, and she had not had anything to eat or drink all day except a cup of coffee early that morning.

"Oh, that's just what I needed," she said to Lydia. "I'm very grateful. Thank you for helping me. I feel better already."

"Good, I'm glad, and you are very welcome," Lydia replied as she sat down beside Taressa. "I'm waiting for my son, Josh. He teaches guitar lessons here on Saturdays. I'm hoping he'll have time to go to lunch with me. Do you have any children?" Lydia had the gift of gab. She never met a stranger, or if she did, they didn't remain strangers very long.

"Uh, no, I don't have any children. I've never married," Taressa explained. "I suppose I've missed out on a lot of joy not having a family of my own, but that's just the way life worked out for me. It would be great if I had a son to go to lunch with, but it wasn't in the cards, I suppose. Is Josh your only child?"

There was the question Lydia never knew exactly how to answer. Should she say "yes" and not acknowledge Mark at all? That didn't seem fair to Mark's memory. Should she say that she has two sons, when that was not entirely true either? How could she tell the whole truth while sparing this lady, who seemed stressed already, the duty of sympathizing with her loss?

Lydia answered Taressa's painful question in the most truthful and positive way she knew how, "I have one son here, that's Josh, and one in heaven. His name is Mark." She spoke the words with a gentle smile, trying to communicate that there was no need for a grim response.

Taressa's eyes almost popped out of their sockets. *Mark Williams . . . the kid killed in Junior's automobile accident . . . I'm almost positive his brother's name was Josh . . . and this lady looks vaguely familiar . . . could it be . . . ?*

Willing herself to speak matter-of-factly, Taressa asked, "Are you by any chance a preacher's wife?"

"Why, yes! My husband is the pastor of Greystone Community Church. How did you know I was a preacher's wife? Have you attended our church?" Lydia inquired curiously.

"Only once," Taressa answered solemnly. "I attended Mark's funeral."

CHAPTER 30

While Janice rested, Casey went through the house looking in every closet, drawer and cabinet, measuring windows for curtains, making note of the colors in each room, and writing up a shopping list for the kitchen and bathrooms. The more she saw, the more she fell in love with Aunt Myra's house, now her own. She wished she didn't have to go back to Greystone at all, but of course she must gather up her clothing and other personal items. She determined that she would move in the following week and start her job search as soon as possible. It was unlikely there would be a teaching position open at this time of year, but not impossible. If nothing else, she could sign up as a substitute teacher or a teacher's aide. That would be a good way to get her foot in the door for next year.

Casey already had her teaching certificate and had, of course, done her practice teaching during her senior year at Easterling. She had not tried to get a teaching job this year because her life was in such turmoil she was not able to focus on her career. Junior's escalating problems which culminated in the accident causing Mark's death and sending Junior to prison, the Marci incident, and her mother's increasing marital and health difficulties had her distracted. She had worked some, part-time, in an upscale boutique in Greystone, selling ladies' clothing and accessories, but it had been little more than an excuse to get out of the house and even less of an opportunity to become independent. Besides, it had become too easy just to rely on Bradley to support her. She realized now that she must become her own person and fulfill the purpose for which God had created her. No more floundering! She was eager to begin teaching elementary children. That had been her career goal since she was a little girl.

Having finished her extensive survey of the house, Casey went into the backyard to see more closely the work that Steven had done. The yard was just the right size. There were enough lawn and flower beds to enjoy, but not enough to require her constant attention to keep them in good shape. Steven had trimmed the shrubs, arranged border bricks around the flower beds, and even installed a simple water feature on the covered patio. What a beautiful place it would be to have coffee while listening to the birds and watching the world wake up early each morning.

The yard was surrounded by a tall cypress fence, so she could not be sure the person she heard puttering around next door was Steven, but she suspected that it was. She owed him a great big "thank you," so she decided to see if it were he.

Casey approached the fence and called out, "Hello, over there. Is that you, Steven?" Of course, she could have peeked through the cracks between the wooden boards, but it would not be good to be caught spying on one's new neighbor that way. Yet, it was very tempting!

"Hi, yourself, and yes, this is Steven. Is that you, Casey?" Steven called back.

"Yes, Steven. Are you very busy? I'd like to speak to you if you can spare a minute," Casey responded.

"I can always spare a minute for a pretty lady. I'll be right there," Steven replied. He came out his gate, stepped over to hers and entered Casey's yard.

Greystone Hearts

He looked different . . . even better than before. He had cleaned up nicely!

"Hi," Steven began the conversation. "I didn't know if you would be back today. What do you think about the house and the yards?"

"That's what I wanted to talk to you about," Casey said. "I love this place! I can hardly wait to move in! I want to thank you for all the yard work you did to get it ready for me. I want to know how much I owe you. Not only have you worked hard, but you spent some money. I want to reimburse you for your expenses and pay you for your time and labor."

"Oh, no, this time it's on me, and it was my pleasure. Mrs. Myra loved to do her own yard work. She was quite an amazing and energetic lady. But when her health began to fail and she was no longer able to continue, I started doing it for her. I never accepted payment."

"Do you mind if I ask why?"

"I had a very good reason. My dad died when I was just a boy, and my mother struggled to rear me alone. Mrs. Myra was like a second mother to me, and she was the reason I was able to go to college. She covered the costs that I couldn't with my scholarships, student loans, and my part-time job. It was a privilege to do something for her in return. Now that the house is yours, you'll want to make your own plans about how to take care of it. But, like I told you and your mother this morning, if you ever need me, all you have to do is call."

"Well, that's very kind of you, and I want you to know I really appreciate it," Casey responded. "When I get settled in, I'd like to have you and your mother over for supper one night so that I can properly express my gratitude. How about it? Do you think you could take a chance on my cooking?" Casey grinned. She was not a good cook, and she knew she would have to find something simple and fool-proof between now and then that she could prepare without creating a disaster. Lucy and Janice did the cooking for the Clemons family, and Casey had spent very little time in the kitchen. Lately, Janice left practically all the cooking to Lucy.

"We'd love that," Steven replied. "You just let us know when you're ready. And, by the way, when you start looking for a church, I'd like you to visit ours, First Baptist Church, Midvale. We have a wonderful church and a great staff. Mother and I would love to have you go with us on a Sunday very soon and check it out."

"Thank you, Steven. I'll look forward to that," Casey answered.

Casey and Steven said their good-byes, and Casey went back into the house, **her** house. She had to keep reminding herself that it was hers, and each time she did her heart skipped a beat. It was almost too much to take in. As she looked around at her new "world" she was thinking, *Oh, God, what an awesome Father You are! I feel Your love all around me. I'm so unworthy of Your goodness, but I love being Your child!*

CHAPTER 31

*R*ichard was a model inmate. He never caused problems and was very respectful toward the guards. Some of the guards were Christian men who felt a certain brotherhood with Richard, despite his heinous crime. They had seen many so-called "jailhouse conversions" in their day. Some of them rang true and were borne out in the behavioral changes they observed. Others were clearly façades to earn favor with the warden and the parole board. Richard was different. He had walked the talk from the very beginning. Even when he was ridiculed and bullied by some of the other prisoners, he had remained civil and controlled in his responses. That's how he had earned the respect of the guards and most of the prisoners he encountered.

One guard in particular was Richard's friend. That friend, Daniel, was the one Richard talked to about the fact that Junior was not receiving all his mail. Daniel discovered the problem, retrieved the letters sent from Rev. Williams that had been withheld by an unscrupulous guard, and delivered them to Junior. Junior read them over and over again and asked Richard to read them as well. Those letters, Casey's letters, Richard's counsel, his own Bible reading, and the working of God's Spirit in his heart were slowly but surely bringing Junior to the brink of surrender.

"I'm sorry about last night," Junior finally broke his silence about the nightmare incident. "I don't know what's going on with me, but maybe you can help me understand."

"I don't know much about dreams," Richard responded. "But I do know that in Bible days God sometimes spoke to people in dreams. Maybe He's speaking to you through your dreams. Why don't you tell me about them, and let's see if we can figure out if there's something to be learned from them?"

"Well, a couple of weeks ago I started having dreams about things that have happened in my life . . . things I've done that I never thought much about before. Most of them I'd totally forgotten. I've always done pretty much what I wanted to do without feeling very guilty about it, but in my dreams the things I did made me feel ashamed. You know what kind of stuff I'm talking about . . . stealing, lying, 'cussing', porn, girls, giving my teachers grief, drinking and drugs . . . you know, just being anything but a Boy Scout! In my dreams I could see myself running around searching to find everybody I'd done wrong over the years and trying to say, 'I'm sorry.' But when I'd find them, they wouldn't listen to me. They wouldn't let me apologize. They'd turn their backs on me and walk away. I'd keep trying to get them to listen, but they didn't seem to think I was sincere, and I could see how much they hated me. After the dreams, I always wake up feeling empty and worthless.

"Last night I dreamed about the wreck. I never have been able to remember much about it because I was so drunk at the time and, I suppose, because my mind just wanted to block it out. But last night I saw the whole thing as though I were up above it, watching it happen in slow motion. I screamed at myself, 'Stop, stop, the light's red!' I felt the impact as our cars collided, and I could see Mark's Nissan go through that plate-glass window. I saw him die. I saw two angels escorting him toward heaven. They passed right in front of my face. I tried to call out to him. I wanted to tell him how sorry I was. I called and called, but he couldn't hear me. Finally, when he and the angels were almost out of sight, Mark turned around and looked straight at me. He reached out his hand toward me and smiled. He didn't say a word, but in my heart I could hear him telling me that he forgave me and that he didn't hate me. It shook me up, and all I could do was cry. I suppose I was actually doing all that screaming and crying out loud when I woke you guys up. What do you make of it?"

"Junior, my guess is that you're beginning to see yourself as you really are. You're a sinner just like everybody else. Perhaps you're getting to the point where you can admit it. Believe it or not, that's a good sign. We're not likely to ask for forgiveness if we don't think we've done anything wrong, just like we don't normally go to a doctor unless we recognize a health problem or need. That's when guilt is a good thing . . . when it brings us to repentance. Repentance means being sorry for what you've done, but it goes one step farther. It means turning away from that way of living and determining to be different with God's help.

"You know, it would be great if all those people you've wronged would forgive you, but more than that you need God to forgive you. If you'll ask Him to, and trust Jesus to save you, He'll do just that. He won't hold your sins against you anymore, and you'll be clean in His sight. I believe Mark was smiling in the dream because he'd taken that step in his life, and he was on his way to heaven. And, because he had been forgiven, he was able to forgive you.

"Junior, we've talked about this many times. When are you going to give it up and ask Jesus into your life to be your Savior too? God has a much better plan for your life than the one you chose for yourself. You made a royal mess of things going it on your own. Why don't you give Him a chance to show you a much better way to live? Give me one good reason why you can't do it right now!"

Junior averted his eyes from Richard's face and stared blankly at the floor. His heart was beating like a bass drum, and he could hardly breathe. The moment of decision had arrived. It was now or, perhaps, never, and he knew it.

"I can't because I don't know how," he humbly answered.

"Well, I can fix that!" Richard responded excitedly and moved from his floor-mounted desk to sit beside Junior on his bunk. "Pray these words after me, but only if you really mean them.

"God in heaven, I'm a sinner. I know I cannot save myself. I repent of my sins. I believe that Jesus died on the cross to pay for my sins. I accept Him as my Savior and Lord. Please accept me as Your child. Forgive me, save me, change me and be my guide through life, and take me to heaven to be with You when I die. Thank You for hearing my prayer and saving me now! Amen."

Richard spoke the words of the prayer in repeatable segments that Junior echoed after him with obvious sincerity. When they lifted their heads and opened their eyes, Junior felt a peace wash over him that he could not describe. He knew in his soul that he was a new person, that he was forgiven, and that he was a child of God. Why, oh, why had it taken him so long to come to this point? His life could have been very different if he had discovered Jesus earlier. Junior could not change his past, but from this time forward, he knew he would never be the same.

Forgiven . . . what a wonderful feeling! Even the air smells cleaner! Junior thought.

"Welcome to the family!" Richard grinned and gave Junior a strong handshake and a big, brotherly hug.

CHAPTER 32

Lydia stared at Taressa questioningly. "Did you know Mark?" she asked.

"No, I didn't know him, but I know Junior Clemons . . . in a way," Taressa replied rather vaguely. In response to the puzzled look on Lydia's face, Taressa continued to explain. "I worked for Bradley Clemons Sr. I was the bookkeeper at Clemons Enterprises. I felt so bad about what happened to Mark I wanted to show my respect and sympathy for your family by going to the funeral."

"Oh, I see. That was very kind of you," Lydia answered softly. "I suppose you're very close to the Clemons family."

"Well, to be honest, I was once too close to Mr. Clemons, but I've had very little contact with his family. Right now, my relationship with Mr. Clemons isn't easy to explain. Let's just say that my job has been terminated, as of today, and we did not part on friendly terms."

"Oh, well, I'm very sorry to hear that. This must be a difficult time for you. We'll just have to pray that God will give you a much better job, and soon!" Lydia spoke encouragingly to Taressa.

"I don't deserve a better job, and I certainly don't deserve your prayers!" Taressa confided.

"What is your name?" Lydia inquired.

"Taressa Tomlinson."

"Taressa, do you mind telling me why you feel that way?" Lydia probed.

"Mrs. Williams, I need a friend right now. You seem like the kind of person who would be understanding and could keep a confidence. I don't want to burden you down with my problems, but do you think there is any way you could help me get out of town discreetly? Bradley Clemons is looking for me, and it's not for a pleasant purpose. I'm afraid of him and with good reason. I'm sorry to draw you into something like this, but I'm rather desperate." Taressa had not really answered the question, nor had she intended to reveal her situation to this woman she barely knew. But, somehow, she felt compelled to trust Lydia with her need.

"Taressa, I'd like to help you, but I must understand what's going on before I can commit to getting involved. Quite frankly, I know that Mr. Clemons has a shady reputation, and I wouldn't want to have any part in his questionable dealings. How do I know that you're not still working for him and involved in something illegal? I just don't know you, and I only have your word to go on. Please understand my dilemma," Lydia reasoned.

"I do understand, Mrs. Williams. Let me tell you what happened to me this morning."

Taressa told Lydia all that had taken place earlier that day at Clemons Enterprises. She explained that she possessed evidence she wanted to get to the FBI concerning Bradley. She pulled the folder out of the tote bag she was carrying and briefly showed Lydia the copied documents it contained.

"Mrs. Williams, I've done wrong. I know I'll be punished for it, but I know I'm doing the right thing now. And, actually, I have no choice any more. Bradley will kill me if he finds me. I need the FBI to protect me from him. If I can just get to a place of safety until I can talk to someone in the FBI, I should be okay. I think they would help me hide from him until I can testify against him in court. Then, I'm willing to take my punishment. That's better than being murdered by Bradley!"

"Who's going to be murdered by Bradley?" Josh interrupted. "What's going on, Mother?"

"Oh, Josh, I came to take you to lunch, but we have more important business now," Lydia answered. "Taressa, I need to tell Josh about your situation. He can help us. Okay?"

Taressa agreed, and Lydia quickly filled Josh in on the basics of Taressa's predicament. Just as she finished, Taressa's cell phone rang. Lydia and Josh waited for her to answer.

"Hello . . . oh, hi, Debra. Thanks for calling me back. Where are you calling from . . . ? Oh, I see. . . . Oh, I'm sorry to hear that . . . . No, don't worry about it . . . I'm okay. My situation is working out. You just take care of yourself and get well soon. I'll be talking to you later. Bye.

"That was my cousin, Debra. I had called her to see if she could come get me. She's in the hospital . . . had back surgery two days ago. I'm striking out everywhere I turn!" Taressa sighed.

Josh looked up in time to see a policeman peering through a large window in the front of Madison's. "Did you say the police are looking for you?" he asked.

"Absolutely!" Taressa responded.

"Well, they may be closing in on you. There's a policeman standing outside Madison's right now. Give me your cell phone!" Josh took the phone and quickly turned it off. Then he hurriedly escorted the two women into his teaching studio, Studio 3, and closed the door behind them.

"Mother, sit here and start playing my guitar and don't stop until I come for you," Josh instructed Lydia.

"But Josh, you know I can't play the guitar. I hardly know which end of it goes up and which goes down!" Lydia exclaimed.

"That's perfect, Mom! You'll sound exactly like one of my beginner students! Just pick away at it and don't worry about how it sounds.

"Miss Tomlinson, you stand in this corner so that if anyone looks through the glass in the door, you'll be out of sight and only Mother can be seen, practicing her guitar! If anyone opens the door, you'll be hidden behind it.

"I'll be back to get you both in just a few minutes, so just stay put until then." Josh gave his orders without wasting time on explanations and then quickly crossed the waiting room area and made for the front door. Once he got there, he took on a nonchalant approach and stepped out the doorway.

"Hi, how are you?" Josh smiled and spoke to the policeman, who seemed to be waiting for someone . . . possibly for backup. "It's a beautiful day, isn't it?" He continued in his carefree manner.

"Yeah, it's a pretty nice day," the cop replied disinterestedly, then continued. "Hey, I'm looking for somebody. Have you seen a redheaded lady around here, or inside the music store, wearing blue slacks and a white sweater?"

"No . . . no redheads that I recall," Josh mused, "except, of course, the little carrot-topped fella' I just finished teaching a guitar lesson. I did see a couple of ladies in the waiting area a little while ago, but one was brunette and the other blonde. I didn't see them there on my way out. I'm curious, though . . . what should I do if I happen to come across this redhead?" Josh asked.

"Call the police immediately, but don't confront her. She may be armed and dangerous. She's a robbery suspect," the policeman replied matter-of-factly.

"Oh, good grief! I'll keep my eyes open. You be careful and have a nice day!" Josh concealed his disbelief and reacted with feigned concern.

Josh sauntered on down the street, pleased that he had been able to truthfully answer the policeman's question without telling all he knew. When he'd gotten about two blocks from Madison's, he watched a florist's van pull into a parking space only a few feet from him. The driver hopped out of the truck carrying a vase of beautiful flowers and walked several yards down the sidewalk before entering the building where, obviously, the floral arrangement was to be delivered. Very discreetly, Josh turned Taressa's cell phone back on. He moved to the back of the van as though going to cross the street. "Accidentally on purpose" Josh dropped a quarter on the pavement and bent down to retrieve it, for the benefit of anyone who might be observing him. As he rose, reclaiming his quarter, he used one hand to brace himself against the florist van's rear bumper. Concealed in that hand was Taressa's small, slender cell phone, which he quickly and inconspicuously tucked behind the license plate far enough to be hidden. The phone fit tightly into the narrow space. Hopefully, it would stay lodged there long enough to be carried far away from where Taressa had last possessed it.

Josh continued quickly to where he had parked his own car that morning. Thankfully, he had chosen to meet with a friend for breakfast in a small café several blocks from Madison's. Then, because it was a nice morning and he wanted the exercise, he had left his car near the café and walked to the music store to begin teaching his Saturday students.

Josh now drove his car around the block and down the alley behind Madison's and parked very close to the rear service door. He sprang out of his car and rang the buzzer that was used to signal when a delivery was being made. One of the clerks came to open the back door. He looked through the peep hole, and there stood Josh. The clerk keyed in the code that disarmed the alarm and let Josh in.

"Hey, man. What are you doing out here?" the clerk inquired.

"I left something in my studio, and I thought it would be quicker to come in through here. Parking spaces are scarce out front, and I'm in a pretty big hurry. Hope you don't mind," Josh explained.

"Oh, no problem. I wasn't very busy. Come on in." The clerk carefully closed the door behind Josh as he entered, and then the clerk returned to the front of the store. Josh hurried to his studio, and when he was sure no one was looking, he hastily escorted Lydia and Taressa into the back room. The policeman was still standing out front when Josh re-entered the code and led Lydia and Taressa, unseen, out the rear service door and into his car. Taressa lay down on the back seat, out of sight.

"Hold on to your wigs, ladies! Here we go!" Josh grinned back at Taressa as he started his engine.

"Where are we going?" Lydia asked Josh, uneasily.

"Where no one would think to look for Miss Tomlinson . . . our house!" Josh replied.

"Why did you take my phone?" Taressa asked from the back seat.

"Well, I suppose I've watched too many crime movies and police shows on television," Josh grinned, "but I've seen where cell phones can be tracked even when they're not in use. I don't know if our Greystone cops have that capability, but you don't need to take the chance. It's possible they've already picked up your signal and know you're in this general area. I don't think they can track it when it's turned off, so that's why I shut it off right away. I turned it back on just before I sent it on a little trip around town. I'm hoping it will lead Clemons and his police buddies off on a wild goose chase. It was just a safety precaution. You can't afford to draw them a map to where you are! We'll get you to our house, and then we'll figure out the next step. Okay?"

"Thanks, both of you! I hope I won't be too big a problem to you. I'll move on just as quickly as I can. I don't want to get you into any trouble," Taressa said.

"Miss Tomlinson, don't worry about us," Josh responded. "I have a feeling you just may be carrying around the answer to a lot of our prayers in that little green tote bag of yours!"

CHAPTER 33

The sun was beginning to set when Janice and Casey returned home to Greystone after their pleasant Saturday in Midvale. They were relieved when they did not see Bradley's canary yellow Porsche Cayman in the garage. That meant they would be free from complaints and condemnations for a little while longer, and no explanations or apologies would be necessary to justify their not being home before he was.

Janice could never really understand why Bradley wanted her to be home when he got there. It wasn't as though he looked forward to a pleasant evening with her. The only explanation she could imagine was that he needed someone with whom to fully vent his anger and over whom to brandish control. It was bad to feel that way about one's husband, but Bradley just seemed to carry around storm clouds wherever he went, and he was never short on lightning and thunder, especially at home.

Lucy had the day off, so Janice and Casey fixed themselves a cup of soup and a salad. After cleaning up in the kitchen, they sat in the den talking about the house in Midvale and Casey's plans to move there right away. Janice was pleased that Casey would have a new life and an opportunity to become independent, but she was also dreading the separation from her beloved daughter. Casey was the one bright spot on Janice's dark horizon. For Casey's sake, Janice must be willing to let her go. This way, when it was Janice's turn to take her leave, it would be easier for Casey to bear.

As soon as Casey moved to Midvale and when Janice was satisfied that Casey was settled and happy in her new life, Janice would make her own move, her ultimate move. Her plan was already in motion; it only had to be tweaked. She did not want to leave any loose ends or any doubts about her actions or her motives. At the rate she was losing strength, Janice figured she may have three to six months of independence left. She could not afford to wait too long, or she would be helpless to retrieve her hidden "escape mechanism" and use it. Six months from today . . . that would be her target, with hope that she would not have to make it sooner. What a strange, scary thing to sentence oneself to death in six months. *So this is what it's like to be on death row with the execution date set!*

****

At almost eight o'clock that Saturday evening, the home phone rang, and Casey answered. "Yes, this is the Clemons residence. Yes, of course, we'll take the call! . . . Junior! How are you? Oh, I'm so glad to hear your voice! We weren't expecting a call tonight. Are you okay?" Casey excitedly took the call from the prison and motioned to her mother that it was Junior. Janice walked as quickly as she could to the kitchen and picked up the cordless phone from there and brought it back into the den so that both she and Casey could talk to Junior together. As she clicked on the phone, Junior had just asked if Bradley was home, and Casey had answered that he wasn't. Junior was unaware that Janice was listening.

"Good," Junior responded. "I wanted some time to talk to you before I talk to him. I think you'll understand why. My cellmate and friend, Richard, was able to get me special permission to make this call. I wanted to tell you what happened to me this afternoon. Casey, I became a Christian too. Richard helped me, and I asked God to forgive me of all my terrible sins, and I accepted Jesus as my Savior. I know you've been praying for me to do that, so I wanted to let you know that your prayers have been answered. I can't tell you how glad I am that you wrote me those letters and that I've finally made my peace with God. I feel like a brand new person. Thank you, Sis, for telling me about Jesus and praying for me. This is the best thing that's ever happened to me!"

Tears were streaming down Casey's face . . . tears of joy. "Oh, Junior, I can't tell you how happy I am to hear this. God is so good! Just think, we really are brother and sister now, in God's family! I love you so much, Junior. We can grow and learn about our new faith together. And there's heaven too! We'll get to spend eternity together in heaven with God when this life is over. Please tell your friend, Richard, 'thanks' for me. Tomorrow I'm going to church at Greystone Community Church. Is it okay if I tell Rev. and Mrs. Williams and Josh about your decision? They've been praying for you too."

"Sure, that would be good! Please tell Rev. Williams that I didn't receive any of his letters until recently. Dad was having them withheld. He didn't want me to 'get religion,' as he puts it. I guess he didn't count on you or Richard putting me on the right track. Anyway, I'm going to write Rev. Williams and his family a letter. I owe them that and a whole lot more. I'll never be able to undo the heartache I brought on them, but if God lets me live and get out of this place someday, I'll do everything I can to show them how sorry I am for what I did to them. For that man to be able to write to me the things he wrote, I knew there had to be a God. Most people would have hated me and God, too, for what happened to their son, but they forgave me before I even asked them to, and they still believe God is good. Well, the guard said I could only talk a few minutes, so I'd better go. Please give Mama Jan a big hug and kiss for me. Tell her I love her, and, Casey, let's start praying for her and Dad to know Jesus too. He's what's been missing in our family all these years."

Janice and Casey stared into each other's faces. Both had tears in their eyes, but Janice didn't speak a word.

"You're absolutely right, Junior! In fact, Mother and I had a short conversation about that this very afternoon. I'm sure we'll be talking about it again very soon. Pray for her!"

Casey and Junior said their good-byes and hung up. Casey turned to her mother and smiled. "You see, I'm not the only one who's found the truth. I know you didn't want to talk about it anymore this afternoon, but would you just give me five minutes to show you a little booklet Rev. Williams gave me that explains very clearly and simply what Junior and I have done? I promise that if you don't want to do what it says, I will leave you alone about it . . . until the next time!" She grinned.

Janice agreed, and Casey went through the small gospel tract with her, explaining the "plan of salvation." When she finished, Casey decided to make the choice as blunt and plain as possible.

"Mother, I'm going to be frank. I'm not going to sugar-coat this at all. You have a choice to make. If all four of us Clemonses were to fall dead in the next thirty seconds, Junior and I would spend eternity together in heaven. You and Bradley would spend eternity together in hell. Is that what you want?"

Janice was speechless. She had never thought of it that way. She didn't really believe in hell, but yet she believed there was a heaven where everyone except extremely bad people went after death. It was her opinion that evil people just ceased to exist. She figured that if she hadn't been good enough for heaven, she simply would "be" no more. But according to the Bible verses in that pamphlet, the only way to heaven was to receive Jesus, and the only alternative was hell. What if she'd been wrong all these years? Having allowed herself only six months (or less) to live, perhaps she had better give this some deep thought. She promised Casey that she would think about it, seriously. She took the gospel tract to her bedroom and placed it on her night stand.

****

Why did she still care? It was pathetic of her to still worry about his safety. He certainly did not concern himself about hers! At what time Bradley had gotten home, Janice was not sure, but it was now eight o'clock on Sunday morning, and she could hear him snoring through his bedroom door. They no longer shared a bedroom and had not for several years. When Janice had turned off the lights and gone to bed shortly after midnight, Bradley had neither come home nor called. She had called his cell phone several times to no avail. Each time she had gotten his voicemail. Her last recorded message said, "Bradley, Casey and I are worried about you. We hope you're okay. Perhaps there's something going on at the plant that has you tied up. It's midnight, and we're going to bed. But if you get this message, please call and let us know you're okay."

It wasn't unusual for Bradley to be out late on Saturday night, but he ordinarily had an excuse and let Janice know not to expect him. That way he didn't have to worry about her calling or trying to locate him. And, from Janice's perspective, she didn't have to wonder if he had driven off a bridge, fallen dead of a heart attack, or choked to death on a big, fat lie! At least he was alive and able to deliver the big, fat lie! Why that still mattered to her, she could not fathom. This time, however, Bradley just didn't want to bother with Janice. He ignored her calls. He was busy looking for Taressa, going to her usual hangouts, calling their mutual friends and acquaintances, keeping in touch with Leonard, combing the streets and driving by Taressa's apartment to see if she had come home.

If Bradley never saw another white car of any kind that would be too soon! After a full afternoon and evening of searching, **the** white Camry had been located sitting alone, after store hours, in a parking lot on Jackson Boulevard where Taressa had abandoned it. The car was parked very near a public bus stop. Bradley figured she had taken the bus downtown.

When Leonard checked out the license plate on the Camry, he discovered that it belonged to a neighbor of Taressa's who lived in the same apartment complex as she. When Leonard called on him to ask about the car, the owner declared that he had lent the car to Taressa because she said hers was not running right, and she needed him to take a look at it. Greg, the helpful neighbor, was a "shade-tree mechanic" and had kept her car to check it out. Taressa had indicated that she needed to borrow his car only for a quick morning errand, but he had not heard from her since, and he had found nothing wrong with her car. He seemed relieved that his vehicle had been found, but concerned about what had happened to Taressa. He was genuinely shocked to learn that his Camry had been used as the get-away car from an armed robbery . . . so said Chief Hatfield!

CHAPTER 34

*P*astor David Williams was about to make his last hospital visit for the day when his wife, Lydia, called his cell phone. "David, come home as soon as possible. There's someone here who urgently needs to talk to you."

"Who is it?" he inquired.

"You'll see when you get here," she said and hung up abruptly. It was not like Lydia to be so curt, and his curiosity was definitely piqued. The best hospital visits, for most patients, are brief ones; so the last visit on David's list today was certainly among the best of the best!

Entering his home by the back door, David found Lydia sharing a sandwich with an attractive, red-haired lady at their kitchen table. Lydia rose from the table and greeted David with a kiss on the cheek.

"David, I want you to meet Miss Taressa Tomlinson. Taressa, this is my husband, David." David stepped forward and shook Taressa's extended hand.

"I'm pleased to meet you, Miss Tomlinson." It was obvious that the puzzled minister was searching his mind for some clue as to who this lady was, why she was here, and if he should recognize her.

"Taressa is, or was, the bookkeeper for Clemons Enterprises for over five years. She's here because she's hiding from Bradley Clemons and the police." Lydia paused for a moment and watched, with a bit of amusement, as David's eyes grew wide and shifted quickly to Lydia.

Answering his quizzical gaze, Lydia proceeded, "David, Taressa has admitted to being involved in some financial dishonesty with Bradley Clemons, but for reasons of her own, she has decided to turn state's evidence and provide proof of those fraudulent business deals to the FBI. Bradley caught her copying the incriminating documents and attacked her. He tried to strangle her, and when she escaped, he reported to the police that she had committed armed robbery at his office, and they're looking for her. She believes that if they find her she will never live to testify against Clemons. She has no place else to go, so Josh and I brought her here. I believe it's providential that our paths crossed at a crucial time and place. Josh has gone back to work. You and I need to help Taressa get in touch with the FBI so that she can put this information into their hands. I think she should stay with us until she knows she's safe. No one would ever consider looking for her here. What do you think?"

"Wow!" David responded. "I feel like we're in a movie scene! But," he added, addressing Taressa, "your life being in danger certainly makes this serious. A lot of people have tried to secure evidence against Bradley Clemons that would hold up in court. Somehow, they've always come up short. It's difficult for me to believe that suddenly substantial evidence has simply fallen into our laps. Taressa, do you mind showing me these papers you have?"

"Not at all, Pastor Williams," Taressa answered without hesitation. "I'll have to explain some of it to you. It may not mean much when you just look at the figures. It's when you compare the falsified reports to the actual invoices and receipts that the truth comes clear. I believe the documents I have could send Bradley to prison for a very long time. I'm afraid I will have to do some time as well, but I'll be safer in jail than I am right now. I'm sorry my problems have intruded into your life. You and your family have already suffered terribly at the hands of the Clemonses. But if you can help me, I will be forever grateful."

Taressa and Lydia finished their lunch, and then Taressa spread out the contents of the folder she had been carrying around protectively in her tote bag. David and Lydia studied the documents carefully and realized that they were, indeed, very damning. David knew exactly whom to call.

At three o'clock Taressa again donned the blonde wig along with the dark glasses, and shortly thereafter David, Lydia and Taressa arrived at the home of Judge Nathan Atwater. Noah Crenshaw of the FBI, along with an agent from the SBI, was waiting there as well. The local police were circumvented because of their connections with Clemons. This investigation was to be conducted and brought to its conclusion by federal and state investigators only. The agents knew that any information given to Greystone's Chief of Police would immediately be passed on to Bradley Clemons, who would then have the opportunity to disappear.

Lydia and David left Taressa with the agents and the judge. The couple drove downtown for Lydia to get her car, which she had left parked near Madison's, and then they went home to take care of the routine get-ready-for-Sunday things that pastors and their wives do on Saturdays.

At seven o'clock there was a knock on their door. Noah Crenshaw stepped into the living room of the Williams home and delivered the update they had been waiting to hear.

"Mr. and Mrs. Williams, I didn't want to say these things over the phone. I thought it best to talk to you face to face. Miss Tomlinson is in the car outside. The windows are darkened and no one can see her. She's in protective custody, and we're taking her to a safe house out of the state. She will be held there until Bradley Clemons is arrested. Just when that will happen, I cannot say for sure. We have to go through proper procedures, but it should be very soon.

"We want to thank you for your co-operation and to stress the importance of total confidentiality in this process. If Bradley Clemons suspects we have Taressa, he'll most likely try to flee the country. We're having him watched to be sure he doesn't get away. Meanwhile, please carry on with your normal activities as though you know nothing of this matter. We'll inform you when the arrest has been made. We expect that when we have Clemons, he will implicate the Chief of Police and others who've been a part of his network. Again, we thank you for your assistance in bringing this man and his cronies to justice. You've performed an important public service for the town of Greystone."

David and Lydia thanked Agent Crenshaw likewise for his helpfulness and his encouraging words to them. They promised confidentiality, sent their regards to Taressa, and Noah left. If the Williams couple had expected to feel thrilled and exhilarated by the recent developments, they were very disappointed. Their emotions were strangely mixed. They were grateful and relieved that an evil person would soon be stopped from hurting others, but they also felt an undeniable sadness that curbed their celebration, sadness for the "lost" condition that had produced such misery in and from one man's life.

CHAPTER 35

Casey came downstairs to have a late breakfast with Janice before dressing for church. "Did Bradley ever come home last night?" she asked her mother.

"Yes, or else another champion snorer is sleeping in his bed right now," Janice smiled. "I don't know what time he got in, though. I woke up off and on during the night, but never heard anything until I got up this morning. He may sleep until noon, but I won't disturb him."

"Well, do you feel like going to church with me this morning? I'm going to visit the Williamses' church and tell them about Junior's phone call last night. I'd love for you to go with me," Casey invited. "I know you feel awkward about meeting them, but I promise they would welcome you. Josh and his dad have invited me several times and asked me to bring you with me."

"To be honest, I just don't feel up to it today. I slept such a little bit last night that I'm extra tired this morning. But I will go with you soon . . . I promise . . . just as soon as I can feel up to it. Besides, I think I'd better be here for Bradley when he wakes up. There's no telling what's going on with him, and he may be upset if I'm not here," Janice replied.

"Are you feeling so bad that you need me to stay with you?" Casey asked.

"Oh, no, not at all, honey. I'm just sleep-deprived. I'll rest some more this morning while Bradley's still sleeping. You go ahead and enjoy your church service. I'll see you at lunch time," Janice insisted.

Casey finished her blueberry muffin, a small carton of yogurt and a cup of coffee before going upstairs to dress for church. At 10:15 she kissed her mother good-bye and headed out to the 10:45 service at Greystone Community Church. Casey had seldom attended church in her lifetime, and she was very excited to be going this morning. She was pleasantly surprised that Janice had promised to go with her in the future. That was a good sign. Perhaps Janice really was beginning to think seriously about spiritual things.

****

Janice took a comfortable feather pillow from her bed and placed it on one end of the sofa in the den. There she lay and relaxed while she waited for Bradley to wake up. She turned the television on and began to channel surf. She scanned right past several channels where various Sunday morning preachers were delivering their sermons, but didn't stop on any of them until she heard a soloist singing a beautiful song that repeated a phrase about coming to Jesus. The stirring song captured her soul with heart-warming words delivered on a heart-melting melody. By the time it was finished, Janice was in tears. She rose from the sofa and went to her laptop computer. When she Googled the recurring phrase, she found several demos of an untitled hymn referred to as, "Come to Jesus," written by Chris Rice. Janice listened to the song sung by its composer several times . . . until she knew what she had to do. In her bedroom, she knelt beside her bed and came to Jesus, crying out for forgiveness and salvation. When she rose to her feet, she felt like singing and dancing to

Jesus, and she knew that when her last breath was taken, she would fly to Jesus.

Janice's eyes fell on the gospel tract that remained on her nightstand and that she had studied several times throughout her restless night. The last page of the booklet read, "Today I asked Jesus to forgive my sins and to become my Savior. Now I belong to Jesus." Underneath that statement was a blank signature line, followed by a line on which to write the date. Janice reached into the nightstand drawer and took out a pen. On the signature line she signed, *Janice Ellis Clemons*. After writing in the date on the second line, she added the time . . . *11:30 a.m.* She could hardly wait for Casey to get home. She smiled as she thought about how happy Casey and Junior would be to learn that their prayers for her were answered so quickly.

In spite of the hard days she knew were ahead for her as she battled a horrific disease, her heart was full of joy and hope. She slipped the tract into her pants pocket and went to the kitchen to begin preparing lunch for Casey, Bradley and herself. As she worked, she hummed the tune to the new song that had spoken distinctly to her heart. Then she began to sing out joyfully an old song she had learned as a small child from her grandmother, before she had been able to fully comprehend its significance, "Jesus loves me, this I know; for the Bible tells me so . . . ." Finally, many years after **learning** those words, Janice **believed** them!

CHAPTER 36

"You sound like a dying calf in a hailstorm!" Bradley scoffed as he staggered into the kitchen, using an old saying he'd picked up from his grandfather to belittle Janice's singing ability. His hair was sticking out in all directions. His face was unshaven. His eyes were bloodshot, and he looked dead on his feet . . . not to mention the big, swollen bruise he bore on the side of his head. "Were you singing about Jesus? For Pete's sake, have you completely lost your mind?"

"Bradley, you look terrible! What in the world has happened to you? How did you get that bruise on your head?" Janice ignored the insult and approached Bradley to take a closer look at his wound.

"Oh, get away! I don't need you making a fuss over a little bruise. Never mind what happened. You wouldn't understand. Is there anything decent to eat around here?" Bradley barked.

"Yes, Lucy left us a nice chicken casserole for today. I was just putting it into the oven to bake. She also left us a tossed salad in the refrigerator." *Lucy, sweet Lucy . . . always thinking ahead and trying to make things easier for me,* Janice thought. "It should take about forty-five minutes for the casserole to bake. If you want something to tide you over, there's still some hot coffee in the coffee pot and a blueberry muffin left from breakfast. How does that sound?"

"I don't like old coffee, fix a fresh pot . . . and I'm not going to wait around for a casserole to bake. I don't want any old leftover muffin, either. I want a **real** breakfast. Fix me two scrambled eggs, bacon and toast. And hurry up with it! I've got to go somewhere. I'm going to get dressed." Bradley snapped out his orders and left the room.

Janice carefully placed the casserole into the preheated oven. She and Casey would have it for their lunch when Casey got home from church. Then she turned her attention to preparing Bradley's "brunch." First, she emptied the coffee pot and started a fresh brew. Then, using the microwave oven to save time, she cooked the bacon and eggs. The toast popped up just as she got the bacon and eggs on the plate. Though she was not as fast and efficient as she had been in the past, she managed to get it all together and placed on the kitchen table nicely arranged on a placemat, with the silverware, napkin, and condiments conveniently positioned by the time Bradley returned. She had done it all in less than twenty minutes . . . quite a feat for her at this stage! When he was seated, Janice brought him a cup of fresh, steaming hot coffee, walking somewhat slowly and cautiously for fear of dropping or spilling it.

"Good grief, woman! By the time you make it to the table with that coffee, it'll be too cold to drink. What in the devil's wrong with you? You know I'm in a hurry! Are you deliberately trying to irritate me?" Bradley grumbled.

"No, Bradley, of course not! I've had a problem with dropping things lately, and I'm just trying to be careful," Janice replied, determined not to become too defensive. She set the cup down near his plate and then sat down in the chair across the table from him. She hoped she might find a way to have a pleasant conversation with him.

"Bradley, I was concerned about you last night. I'm glad you got home safely, although, from the looks of that bruise, you barely made it. When you get through with whatever you've got to do today, do you think we could spend a little time together, maybe go for a drive, or go out to dinner, or just watch a little television? I'd love it if we could be together more, like a real married couple."

"Janice, don't start in on me. I can't stand that nagging. If you like living in this fine house, driving that Mercedes and having all those nice clothes hanging in your closet, then you'll just have to accept the fact that somebody's got to work to pay for it. One thing's for sure . . . you never bring a penny into this house . . . all you do is spend!" Bradley growled.

"I don't mean to nag, Bradley. I appreciate all the good things you work hard to provide for me. I truly do. I just want us to get along better and try to improve our marriage. I think we could do that if we spent some time together and worked at it a little more. What would be wrong with that?"

"I like our marriage just the way it is," Bradley retorted sharply. "If you don't, then you're free to leave. I don't need or want a mushy, sentimental relationship. I'm not that kind of guy, and I don't want to hear any more about it."

"Well, Bradley, I never thought I'd say this, but I just might take you up on that offer to 'leave if I want to.' Would you really let me go?"

Bradley laughed uproariously. "Oh, yeah? And where would you go? What man would have you with all your petty ailments? You know you've never held a real job in your life. And don't even think about alimony. I'll fight you tooth and nail if you try to get anything from me! You couldn't make it six months on your own!"

Janice chuckled inside at the last statement. "Actually, I'd settle for six months of peace and happiness," she grinned knowingly. "Besides, Bradley, you could be wrong. I just might surprise you. It's possible that I'm not as inept and stupid as you think I am. As a matter of fact, I'm quite sure a trial separation is just what we need."

A surge of boldness had come over Janice that she could hardly believe. Surprisingly, she was no longer afraid of her husband! She . . . a weak, diseased, dying woman had more strength and courage at this moment in her life than she had ever possessed when she was healthy and vibrant. She stood up from her chair, straightened herself to her full height, gave Bradley a brief, unwavering stare, turned deliberately and walked with as much poise as she could muster from the kitchen to her bedroom without another word to Bradley. As she made her exit she triumphantly hummed her new favorite tune!

Bradley stopped in mid-chew and watched in amazement as Janice left him alone in the kitchen wondering what she meant by "trial separation."

*Just chew on **that** for a little while, Mr. 'I'm not that kind of guy!'* Janice thought.

CHAPTER 37

Casey entered the sanctuary of Greystone Community Church about fifteen minutes before the worship service was to begin. Bible study classes were just letting out, and the praise team and band had just finished their warm-up rehearsal. Josh had rejoined the group and was again at his post on stage with his guitar when he spotted Casey entering the worship center. He made his way down from the platform and hurried to greet and welcome her.

"How are things going for you, Casey?" Josh inquired.

"Well, some things never change, like Bradley, but other things have changed dramatically," Casey replied. She proceeded to tell him about Junior's telephone call the night before.

"Oh, that's wonderful news!" Josh exclaimed. "My parents are going to be overjoyed. They've been praying for this. They've wanted something good to come out of Mark's death, and what could be better than snatching a soul off the path to hell and putting him on the road to heaven?"

"Make that two souls! My soul got 'snatched' too!" Casey grinned. "And I will always be grateful to you and your family for not shutting Junior and me out of your hearts when you had every right to do so. We will never be able to thank you enough." Casey's eyes teared up as she poured out her gratitude.

"If I've learned anything from this whole experience of losing my brother, Casey, it's that forgiveness is a God thing, and it has the potential for all kinds of positive ripple effects." Josh smiled knowingly as he reflected on how difficult it had been for him to get past seeking revenge.

Casey then told Josh briefly about her home in Midvale and her plans to move into the house the next day. Josh was, again, very happy for her.

When Lydia entered the sanctuary, Josh introduced her to Casey. Lydia invited Casey to sit with her during the worship service. The two women liked one another immediately.

Soon the organist began to play, and people who had been milling about speaking to one another and exchanging hugs made their way to their pews and began to settle into a mood of worship. Casey was surprised to see two television cameras and their operators preparing to broadcast the service over the local television station. She was totally unaware that Greystone Church had begun televising its Sunday morning worship services about six months earlier.

Casey sat beside Lydia and enjoyed the music by the praise team, choir, and instrumentalists as well as the powerful and inspiring sermon delivered by Pastor Williams. But the part of the service that surprised and touched her most was when Josh stepped to the pulpit just before his father preached and sang the most beautiful and moving song she had ever heard. It touched her heart deeply, and she was amazed at how beautifully Josh sang it.

As Casey listened in awe to the message of the song, she thought, *Oh how I wish Mother could hear this! I just know it would touch her heart, too.* It was a song that invited everyone to come to Jesus and live.

****

Janice remained in her room until she heard Bradley leave the house very shortly after their conversation. Then she returned to the kitchen to check on the casserole baking in the oven. While she was waiting for Bradley to leave, she had begun going through her closet and dresser drawers selecting enough clothing to get her through the next week at least. She could come back someday when Bradley was not at home to get more of her things, but she was determined to be gone before Bradley returned today. She expected he would be gone all afternoon and evening, so there was plenty of time, she thought.

At about twelve-thirty, Casey came home from church. She was full of enthusiasm over the worship service and her time with the Williamses and eager to tell Janice all about it. But Janice was just as intent on sharing her own experience.

When Casey joined her mother in the kitchen, Janice said, "Let's fix our plates and sit down together. I've made two major decisions this morning, and I want to tell you about both of them." Casey could see the fervor in Janice's eyes and waited eagerly to hear what she had to say.

Mother and daughter seated themselves at the table. When Casey had thanked the Lord for their food, the beginning of a new practice, Janice pulled the gospel tract from her pocket and handed it to Casey.

"Read the last page, please," Janice instructed. Casey flipped to the back of the booklet and read the signed and dated acknowledgement that Janice was now a believer. Casey could hardly believe her eyes. She jumped excitedly from her chair and zipped around the table to hug her mother.

"Mother, that's terrific. I want to hear all about it!" Casey exclaimed.

Janice told Casey how she had kept waking up in the night. She believed it was due to a combination of excitement over their wonderful Saturday together, plus concern for Bradley, plus a feeling of urgency to act on the things Casey had shared with her about Jesus. Each time she woke up she would listen to hear if Bradley had come in, and then she would read through the little gospel tract she had placed on her nightstand.

Then Janice told Casey about the amazing song she'd heard on the television and afterward Googled on the Internet and how it had helped her to finally pray to Jesus for forgiveness and salvation.

Casey listened in amazement. She could hardly believe it. It must have been Josh that Janice had heard singing that song on television. The lyrics Janice quoted were the same as those Josh had sung. It was simply uncanny how the Williams family continued to bless the very family that had devastated theirs. *Yes, indeed,* Casey pondered, *forgiveness **has** to be a God thing! And the ripple effects are awesome!*

****

While Janice and Casey were having lunch and conversation together at home, Bradley was having a beer and conversation with Chief of Police Leonard Hatfield at a "greasy spoon" near Clemons Garment Factory.

"I want to know what you've found out about Taressa since we talked last!" Bradley demanded. "Were you able to track her cell phone?"

"Bradley, she made her last call from somewhere downtown. Since then we followed the signal here and there until it stopped. We found the phone in the middle of 15th Avenue where it had apparently been run over by a vehicle and was smashed to pieces. Don't ask me how it got there or where she is, but we're combing the area where the phone was found. So far, we've got nothing. She just vanished."

"Well, that's just great! You let her get away! There's no telling where she is or who she's 'singing' to. You did a fine job, Leonard!" Bradley seethed sarcastically. "What am I supposed to do now . . . just sit around here and wait to get arrested?"

"Bradley, you're over-reacting! Taressa's not singing to anybody! She's an accomplice, and she'd be signing her own arrest warrant. Don't you see that you just scared her half to death? You should never have attacked her! You could have paid her off and worked things out if you had controlled that temper of yours. Just give her a little time to calm down. I expect she'll contact you and try to work out a deal where she can go away quietly with a comfortable little severance package, and that will be the end of that. Trust me on this. You're going to be okay!" the not-so-sharp Leonard insisted.

"That's fine for you to say, Leonard. You don't have anything to do with Clemons Enterprises, so she's got nothing concrete on you there. However, let me remind you that if I get nailed for **anything**, you're definitely going to feel my pain. I'll sing the curtains down about how you have your finger in the pie with the extra-curricular activities going on at the plant. You haven't exactly been looking the other way for free. And don't forget how you botched up the investigations when I did what I had to do to get the properties I needed for the plant. I lined your pockets nicely for that. I can put you away for a very long time, and don't think I won't!

"And, there's one thing you aren't considering about Taressa. She's a 'woman scorned' and full of hell's fury. She found out about my newest lady friend, and she's capable of doing anything to make me pay for dumping her. She actually believed that I was going to divorce Janice and marry her. I think she'd be perfectly satisfied to go to prison just to put me there! So don't try to soothe things over with your flimsy philosophies. I know her a lot better than you do!

"Now, listen. I've got bank accounts out of the country, so I think I need to cut my losses and get lost overseas while the getting is good. Your job is to help me do it, because if I'm not safe, neither are you. I need a new name and some fake ID. I know you have sources and can make that happen, so get on it now. I'm leaving the country as soon as possible. Don't let me down!"

Bradley abruptly got up from his chair and stormed out, leaving Leonard in the biggest pickle he'd ever experienced. As he watched Bradley leave the café in a huff, Leonard's wheels began to turn, and he sneered as he thought. *My life would be a whole lot simpler without you in it! If I could get hold of those foreign accounts, I'd be very tempted to eliminate you and retire! Even without the money, I don't plan on letting you send me to prison. You just think you're in control here, my friend. I don't like being threatened, and I'm through taking orders!*

CHAPTER 38

"Now, tell me about that second important decision you made today!" Casey asked her mother as they continued their Sunday lunch together.

"Well, Casey, that decision is not such a happy one as the first, but I believe it's necessary. You know how hard I've tried to make my marriage work with Bradley. What we have is not really a marriage at all, and he doesn't want to change the way it is. He's been unfaithful to me many times with many women. Soon after our wedding, I realized that Bradley married me just to have someone to take care of Junior while he chased wealth and women. I was chosen for that assignment simply because I was in the wrong place at the wrong time, and Junior had formed an attachment to me as his substitute mother.

"This morning I told Bradley that I'm going to separate from him for a while. It may be permanent, depending on if he decides he can change. I'm going to get a room at a hotel for a few days until I can find an apartment. I have some money put back that I've saved over the years from what Bradley gives me for household operating expenses, and that will get me by until I can see what's going to happen. If it's divorce, I will sue for alimony, and, whether he likes it or not, he'll have to pay. I have grounds, and I have evidence. He can't pay off every lawyer and judge around. He just thinks he can."

"Mother! You'll do no such thing! Why on earth would you get an apartment and live alone when you could live with me in Midvale? That's simply out of the question. I wouldn't have that house at all if it were not for you. That home is still as much yours as it is mine, as far as I'm concerned. I don't care whose name is on the deed, that's **our** house . . . yours and mine! You're coming with me to Midvale, and that's settled!

"I'm sorry, in a way, that you and Bradley are separating, but I can certainly understand why you feel you must. I've watched him mistreat you all these years, and I know it has only gotten worse. You're not in the best of health, and that makes his behavior even harder to take. I want us, you and I, to start a new life together. I want to take you to a new doctor and see if we can't find out why you're not getting better. I'm afraid I've lost confidence in your current doctor, and I actually believe that living under Bradley's suppression has contributed to your health problems. What do you say? Will you go with me?" Casey pled persuasively.

"Casey, I would love nothing better, but I'm determined not to be a drag on your life. You don't need an ill mother to worry about. Believe me, I would become a burden. I want you to be free," Janice responded with a lump in her throat.

"Let me see if I understand you, Mother. You brought me into this world, took care of me day and night when I couldn't do a thing for myself, watched over me and did your very best for me for twenty-three years, and just yesterday you gave me a lovely home and a chance to start a new life. Now, when you need me, I'm supposed to let you go off alone so that you won't inconvenience me? I don't think so!"

"But you don't understand all the facts, Casey," Janice replied. She had not wanted to tell Casey the whole truth, but now it seemed inevitable. It was time to face the facts and allow Casey to do the same. "Casey, I'm not going to get any better. My doctor's not at fault. I've kept the truth from you, trying to protect you. Casey, I have ALS, better known as Lou Gehrig's disease. I've known it for several months now, and I've exhibited symptoms for much longer. It takes a while to diagnose. They had to rule out a lot of other things before finally discovering my real problem. At best, with some physical therapy and good care, I may have another three years to live but the quality of my life during that time will diminish steadily. I'll go from a walker, to a wheelchair, to being totally bedridden. Then it will take feeding and breathing tubes to keep me alive. But it won't be any kind of life that I would want to prolong. How quickly all this will happen, I can't know. Every case is different, but the ultimate outcome is the same.

"It's a horrible disease, the worst I can imagine. When I first found out, I planned to take my own life while I had the strength to do it. I was going to take poison while I could still swallow. There will come a time when I can no longer do that. At the end, my muscles will be so weakened I may not even be able to blink my eyes.

"That's why I was so happy that Aunt Myra left me that house and I could give it to you and see to it that you were on your own and doing well before I took a poisonous dose of cyanide. All that has changed now. I'm going to trust God to get me through and meet my needs. Perhaps He will spare me the worst of the suffering. I've read that often ALS patients die of secondary infections, especially of the lungs, before they reach the final stages of ALS. I would consider that a gift of God's mercy if He allows that to happen to me. But until whatever takes me out, I want to live each day to the fullest, and, most of all, I want you to be happy. I'm sorry to drop this bombshell on you, honey, but you had to know eventually."

As she absorbed the news of her mother's devastating disease, Casey's emotions took a sudden plunge from the mountaintop to the lowest valley. She and Janice embraced and cried until there were no more tears to shed. Then they began to look to the future and decide on a plan.

"Mother, I choose to believe that you have a significant amount of good time left, and you're going to spend it with me. When the bad time comes, I'll get whatever help I need to take care of you. During the worst time, if it gets to the point that you can't be comfortable at home, I'll find a place where you'll get the very finest professional care. But the most important thing for you to know is that as long as I'm alive and able, you'll be cared for in the best possible way.

"I don't want you to be afraid. We have a heavenly Father who understands our trouble, and He'll be with us all the way. The truth is we don't know what the future holds. Something could happen, and we both could be gone in an instant, just like Mark Williams. We only have the present, so let's just take it one day at a time, do the best we can, and trust God for the rest.

"Now, I've finished my sermon. Let's get packing! I say we should go to Midvale today. Dogwood Lane, here we come!"

CHAPTER 39

After his meeting with Leonard Hatfield, Bradley went to his office at Clemons Enterprises to retrieve some papers he needed to take with him when he made his escape. Other documents, he shredded. Then, from his private safe, to which no one else knew the combination, he took a pouch full of cash, enough to serve him very well until he could get to his foreign accounts. Then he took out his handgun and undercover shoulder holster. He removed his jacket and strapped on the holster. After making sure the revolver was fully loaded, he slipped it into the holster and put his jacket back on over it. When he finished his errands and was ready to leave the office, he took a long look around and sighed deeply as he realized his empire was crumbling down around him, all because of a redhead. How he hated her! How he wished he could find her and finish the job of strangling the life out of her! And oh how he wished he could know for sure if she had squealed!

What if Leonard were right and Bradley was throwing it all away needlessly? Should he take the chance? Perhaps, once he got to a safe place, he could wait to see what happened. If nothing came of it, he could return and pick up where he left off. Yes, maybe he could arrange for it to look as though he were going away temporarily on business. He could monitor the situation from a safe distance and come back when the storm blew over. Junior should be getting out of prison before long, in about three months at the most if his parole came through . . . and why wouldn't it? It would be nice to be home and have all this mess straightened out by then.

Bradley called the garment plant manager and the managers of each of the other establishments he owned that together formed Clemons Enterprises. He told them all that he had urgent business out of town and did not know when he would be back. He explained that he'd caught Taressa stealing and had been forced to fire her; so the office would be closed until he could return and find a replacement for her. Meanwhile, they were to conduct business as usual and keep up with their paperwork. Things would return to normal as soon as possible.

Good, he had left his options open! Perhaps he could save his empire despite his fears. He was beginning to feel a bit hopeful. Maybe he had just been paranoid, after all. Still, his gut told him to "get out of Dodge" until he could learn more about Taressa's intentions and activities.

After making plane reservations for New York City, he headed home to pack. He should be able to get lost in a city that large for quite a while. Then, if he needed to fly out of the country, he would, from New York. By then Leonard should have him fixed up with his new identity.

Driving home, he noticed a blue car in his rear-view mirror that looked familiar. Where had he seen that car lately? Was he being followed? There was one way to find out. Bradley drove carefully at the legal speed limit trying to appear unaware of his pursuer, but began to make a series of turns that made no sense at all. He was virtually going in circles, and the blue car followed a little distance behind him. He broke out in a cold sweat when he went through a yellow light and then observed the blue car do the same even as the light was turning red. *Too late,* he thought. *They've got me. I should have run last night.*

Suddenly, the blue car turned into a driveway. Bradley was stopped at a two-way stop sign. He waited and watched closely in his side mirror as a young mother got out of the driver's seat and then removed an infant in its carrier from the back seat. Bradley felt totally foolish. He had nearly worked himself up into a heart attack over nothing. *So this is what it will be like as long as I stay around here,* Bradley thought. *I can't live like this. It's settled . . . I'm leaving for good!*

****

"Layup vehicle no longer in command of target. Spotted. Activate backup vehicle," Agent Jody Gibbs reported through her communications device within the blue sedan.

"Okay, Alpha. Charlie's right behind you. Bravo's in advance position. Target is still in the box."

The FBI's vehicle surveillance team had Bradley covered. It was obvious to the agent in the command vehicle that Clemons was probably headed home. Bradley had only spotted the blue sedan in the "box" of various vehicles being used to track him. The arrest warrant had been issued, and they could pick him up at any time now, but his home would be the preferred location.

The informant sent word that Bradley was making plans to leave town and the Bureau had just discovered he'd bought a plane ticket for New York City, leaving in the morning. That information made concerns about losing him less, but not nil. The sly fox may have bought the ticket as a ploy, and could be on his way out of town, in his automobile, at this moment. They must not take anything for granted.

Agent Gibbs grinned as she looked back at the amazingly realistic doll wrapped in a blue blanket and secured snugly in its baby carrier that was again strapped safely to the back seat of the blue sedan. *Works every time!* she mused.

****

Leonard was busy too, but not acquiring fake ID. He called off all the illegal gambling and prostitution that had been operating from the garment factory and told everybody to lie low until they heard from him, and to keep their mouths shut. "Business" was suspended indefinitely. They were in danger of being exposed. In fact, if they could leave town for a while that would be even better.

Leonard had suddenly found new evidence that Bradley was connected with the burning of Tom Wong's dry cleaners. Strange how things like that can happen long after the fact! But Leonard obtained a quick arrest warrant for the arsonist who had been paid by Clemons to burn the place down. Leonard had arranged for the unsuspecting arsonist, who was convinced his crime was long forgotten, to be picked up, booked and jailed. Now, Leonard had the sad task of arresting his friend, Bradley Clemons. It was something he preferred to do alone . . . supposedly to spare Bradley the embarrassment of an audience of officers. He was sure he could persuade Bradley to surrender peaceably, so that it would appear Bradley had turned himself in voluntarily, and there would be no trouble.

"Bradley, I've got what you wanted. I'm on my way to your house, about two or three minutes away. Where are you?" Leonard inquired of Bradley over his cell phone.

"I'm about ten minutes away. I'll meet you there. If somebody's home to let you in, wait for me in my study and don't breathe a word about any of this to Janice or Casey," Bradley instructed, extremely pleased that Leonard had been able to obtain the fake ID that quickly. Maybe Leonard was smarter than Bradley thought!

CHAPTER 40

Leonard rang the doorbell. Casey left off packing and ran down the stairs to answer the door. She was not exactly surprised to see the chief; he was a friend of Bradley's and an occasional visitor. But this call was unexpected and untimely.

"Hi, Chief Hatfield, I'd invite you in, but my step-father isn't home. I'm afraid I don't know when to expect him, either." Casey did not want company to slow down the packing project, and she had never felt comfortable around Leonard anyway. She hoped he would go away.

"Oh, that's okay, Little Miss. I just talked to him on the phone. He'll be here in about five minutes. He wants me to wait for him in the study. You don't mind, do you, Little Miss?"

Casey hated it when he called her that. Just something about the condescending way he said it made her skin crawl. She didn't answer the question, but simply said, "Oh, in that case, let me show you to the study."

Casey led Leonard to the study and offered him a seat. "I hope you'll excuse me, Chief. I'm in the middle of an important project upstairs, and I really need to get back to it. Do you mind waiting here alone for Bradley?"

"Why no, Little Miss. You go right ahead about your business. I'll be just fine." Leonard was actually glad to be left alone in Bradley's study. He got up and closed the study door, and with an ear kept sharply tuned to hear Bradley come into the house, he began to rummage through Bradley's desk. How sweet it would be if he happened to come across information that would enable him to pilfer Bradley's foreign bank accounts. After all, if his plan succeeded, Bradley would have no use for all that money.

To his great disappointment, Leonard was only able to access one drawer, the one seemingly filled with nothing more than ordinary desk supplies. All the other drawers were locked. He would have been caught searching through the top drawer had it not been for Janice. She had stepped into the hallway outside her bedroom, and she saw Bradley coming in the front door. Just before he reached the study she called out to him.

"Bradley, I need to speak to you for a minute, please," Leonard heard her say.

Bradley paused for just a moment and replied, "Not now, Janice. I'm busy. Leonard's here on business. I'll talk to you when we finish up."

Leonard just barely had time to shove the drawer closed, scurry back to his chair and assume an expression of angelic innocence before Bradley flung open the door and met his gaze. Bradley turned back to Janice as he began to shut the door again and said, "Janice, I'm not to be disturbed, understood?"

"Yes, Bradley, I understand," Janice replied.

Bradley shut the door, locked it and walked across the room to his desk. He seated himself in his plush, leather office chair behind the desk. "Well, let's have it! Show me what you've got," he insisted, wasting no time.

The moment had come. If he played his hand just right, he could make it look like Bradley had resisted arrest so that he had been forced to take him at gun point. Then, when he was attempting to cuff him, Bradley tried to grab the gun, and it went off.

Poor Bradley. The bullet would go right through his heart. *So sorry . . . unavoidable . . . he was my friend . . . tried to make the arrest as painless as possible . . . blah, blah, blah!* Leonard was prepared. That would be his story, and he'd be sticking to it! But there was no room for error. He had to do it right . . . just the way he had played it out in his mind. His scheming heart was racing.

Unbeknown to Leonard and Bradley, four FBI agents had driven up to the house immediately after Bradley entered. Janice saw two of the men approaching the front door as she left the study and walked into the living room. They passed by the picture window where the drapes were open, and she knew they were about to knock or ring the doorbell. Janice mistook them for men from Bradley's business club. But Bradley had asked not to be disturbed . . . no, not "asked" . . . demanded, so she ran interference by opening the door before the two, suit-and-tie-clad gentlemen had an opportunity to ring the doorbell. She greeted them with a congenial smile.

"Hello, how may I help you?"

"Are you Mrs. Bradley Clemons Senior?" one of the men replied.

"Yes, I am."

"Ma'am, we need to see your husband."

"Well, I'm terribly sorry. This is a bad time. He's in a meeting and has asked not to be disturbed. Could you just leave your card or your contact information? I'll ask him to get in touch with you as soon as possible after his meeting."

"No, ma'am, I'm afraid we can't do that. This is a very urgent matter, and we must insist on seeing him. Please tell him we're waiting and wish to speak to him immediately." The men stood their ground, and Janice sensed that something important was about to take place. These men, though quite polite, looked very serious. She was afraid it meant bad news.

"Well, please step in and have a seat. I'll go see if I can get him to come out and talk to you." Janice directed the men toward the living room. The men stepped into that room, but declined to sit, instead stating that their business would only take a couple of minutes and that they preferred to stand while they waited. Their unspoken motive was so that when Janice walked away to call Bradley they could step to a place where they could better observe any movement in that area of the house, in case Bradley were to try to leave. They must be in a position of readiness and expecting the unexpected.

Janice nodded in assent to their preference and stepped down the hall to the study door.

Meanwhile, in response to Bradley's request for the identity documents, Leonard tossed an envelope onto Bradley's desk and then stepped back away from the desk, in close proximity to the locked door behind him. Bradley reached for the envelope, tore into it and began reading the arrest warrant issued in his name which accused him of conspiracy to commit arson and related offences.

"What kind of joke is this?" Bradley hissed, tossing the affidavit back across the desk toward Leonard.

"No joke at all, my friend." Leonard sneered as he drew his weapon and pointed it at Bradley. "I'm not your puppet anymore. From now on, you take orders from me. Now, put your hands behind your head and stand up. You're under arrest, and you're going with me." Leonard intended to let Bradley get close to him and then to shoot him through the heart. He would later pretend they had struggled for the gun and that it had gone off accidentally.

But Janice's timing was freakish. She knocked on the study door and began announcing that Bradley had visitors on urgent business. Once again, Janice was in the wrong place at the wrong time . . . or was she? The interruption startled Leonard, whose nerves were already wound tight, and he impulsively looked toward the door, forgetting that it was locked and fearing that Janice would walk into the room. That brief interval of distraction afforded Bradley, now standing behind his desk with both hands placed on the back of his head, the opportunity to whisk his revolver from its holster and fire at Leonard. But Leonard saw the movement in his peripheral vision as Bradley lowered his hand and thrust it under his jacket for the gun, and he dove to the floor. The bullet from Bradley's gun barely missed Leonard and pierced the study door.

With Leonard on the floor, scrambling for cover behind a large chair while simultaneously trying to get a bead on Bradley, Bradley saw his opportunity to escape. Crouching behind his massive desk, he flung the drapes aside that covered the French doors behind him, reached up and quickly turned the latch that unlocked the deadbolt, and then lunged through the open doors . . . practically plunging into the arms of the other two FBI agents who were covering the back of the house. Both agents had their guns drawn and aimed squarely at Bradley.

"Drop the gun, now!" The agents shouted. Bradley stood frozen in his tracks. Dismally realizing the futility in resisting, he slowly lowered his weapon to the ground.

"Step away from the gun," was the next order he received and obeyed.

"Now, get down on the ground with your hands behind your head!" Again, Bradley complied.

Inside the house, the two agents Janice had greeted ran to the study when they heard the gunshot. One of the agents stopped to examine Janice who lay on the floor in front of the study door while the other burst through the door and caught Leonard as he was trying to escape through the window and issued the same orders to him that Bradley had received.

Casey heard the gunshot from upstairs and came running down the steps in a panic. When she saw her mother lying on the floor, she became hysterical. The agent attending Janice tried to calm Casey and called for an ambulance. Janice was bleeding profusely and turning very pale. The bullet had penetrated the door and entered Janice's chest. It appeared that perhaps an artery had been severed.

Casey knelt beside her mother and begged her to live. Her voice trembled with fear and disbelief as she tried to take in the scene. She had been totally unaware that the two agents were in the house to see Bradley and could not understand what was happening. Nor did the agents understand exactly what had happened in the study. But the pressing issue now was to get help for Janice.

Two of the agents cuffed Bradley and Leonard, read them their rights and took them to the car. There would be time for questions and answers later.

Janice opened her eyes and stared up at Casey. She could feel the life slowly but certainly seeping out of her, yet she felt an overwhelming sense of peace. She had no fears or worries about herself, only regret for the panic she saw in the face of her child.

"It's okay, sweetheart. No matter what happens, it's okay because I'm ready. I'm ready to go home. Please, don't be too sad. I'll be there waiting for you, and for Junior too. I love you both with all my heart."

Janice's words grew faint, and her grip on Casey's hand loosened as her voice trailed off. She managed a slight smile as her eyes slowly closed for the last time, and Janice flew to Jesus.

EPILOGUE

(About eighteen months later)

Now there are two men named Bradley Clemons in the same prison. One, the younger man, could have been released on parole more than a year ago, but chose to serve out his three year sentence. Surprisingly, the Williams family had volunteered to speak to the parole board on his behalf, but the young man wanted to do his time and then be free from probation requirements. Besides, he felt he owed it to the memory of Mark Williams to complete his sentence.

The other Bradley Clemons, the elder one, will be a very much older man before, and if, he ever walks the streets of Greystone, or any other city, again. He was convicted of a long list of white collar crimes, plus other offenses including operating a prostitution ring, sponsoring illegal gambling, conspiracy to commit arson, attempted murder (of Leonard Hatfied), and (saddest of all) the manslaughter of his wife. Bradley's chickens finally came home to roost. He would much prefer being back in an old, trashy trailer on Tanner Road to his present address.

Former Chief of Police, Leonard Hatfield, is adjusting to confinement as well. He will be out before Bradley, but he, too, will be quite past his prime. Meanwhile, Greystone is flourishing under the protection of a tightened-up police force led by the new Chief of Police, Reggie Green.

Taressa Tomlinson, the attractive redhead, the bookkeeping partner in crime, the lover spurned, received a three-year suspended sentence and moved away to start a new life, an honest life, vowing never to cheat in business or love again.

Richard Levitt continues to serve his Lord while he serves his sentence, sharing the gospel with the men in prison alongside him. Now, and for a little while longer, he has a young assistant.

"Uncle Sam" got his back taxes plus penalty payments from confiscated funds. From the remaining Clemons wealth, the NBC Prayer Club members and others defrauded by Bradley Clemons were compensated. Some of them chose to accept interest in Clemons Garment Factory (now renamed Greystone Garment Factory) in lieu of cash settlements. The plant is running smoothly, still providing honest jobs for honest workers under the supervision of a capable board of directors, on which Junior Clemons (now called "Brad") will hold a prominent position when released. Nobody works the night shift at the plant anymore, except the night-watchman!

Clarence Brown took his cash settlement and built himself a new Corner Café, but on another corner. The newspaper carried a large color photo of Corner Café Two alongside a front-page story describing how the former Corner Café had been unjustly maligned and promoting the new establishment. Business is booming!

Jasper Morris (the bus driver), Tom Wong, and others in the NBC Prayer Club kept their current jobs but now enjoy much greater financial security with their settlement packages stored away in the bank or invested other places.

The four businesses making up Clemons Enterprises were purchased outright at very obliging prices by their individual managers and are now independent, thriving establishments. Clemons Enterprises has become a mere smudge on the pages of Greystone's history.

Josh and Marci are newlyweds. Josh teaches history and is an assistant coach at Greystone High School. On the side, he continues to teach guitar, and Marci teaches piano at Madison's. Together they play for special events in the tradition of Josh and Mark, and they serve joyfully in the music ministry of Greystone Community Church.

David Williams continues to faithfully pastor his church, and Nathan Atwater remains an honest judge. Their wives, Lydia and Betty, are close "in-law" friends and look forward to the days when they will share grandbabies.

Casey Ellis (Clemons no more!) is becoming a strong young woman living alone on Dogwood Lane, staying in close contact with "Brad," teaching third grade in Midvale, growing in her faith, singing in the choir at First Baptist Church, recovering from the loss of her beloved mother (Janice) and falling more in love every day with Steven, who will soon finish law school. Daisy has become a close friend and a "second mother" to Casey. All their friends predict it won't be long before Casey becomes Daisy's daughter-in-law.

Mark Williams is remembered with love, and his memory is honored through a music scholarship established in his name and presented annually to a deserving music student at Halford-Easterling College.

All the "players" that touched the hearts of Greystone for good are amazed at how God continues to fit together the tiny puzzle pieces of their lives to show His glory and to knead their sorrows into blessings. He's famous for that!

One more thing! When Bradley Clemons Senior finally had his day in court and was convicted of all the charges brought against him, and shortly after he was taken from the local jail to state prison, he received a letter. He opened the envelope and cursed the contents. Yes, another jail cell drawing! Only this time there was no poem. It simply announced, "**Justice is served!**" AND, it was signed . . . *Luke and Lucy.*

AUTHOR PAGE

Linda Kay DuBose, a former schoolteacher, is the wife of a minister and has two children and eleven grandchildren. She is a graduate of William Carey University in Hattiesburg, Mississippi. This is her second novel. A native of Laurel, Mississippi, she now resides with her husband Wayne in Shreveport, Louisiana.

****

Thank you for reading Greystone Hearts. I invite you to visit my author page on Amazon where you may leave a brief review, see my other titles and/or enter a discussion about any of my books. LKD

Amazon.com/author/lindakaydubose

Other books by Linda Kay DuBose

ERVE AND LIZZIE
SOMEDAY, MAYBE…FOR SURE!
EMERALD MIST

Made in the USA
Columbia, SC
27 October 2020